THE
PHANTOM
QUEEN

Edited by Geoffrey Ursell.
Cover painting and interior illustrations by Aries Cheung.
Cover and book design by Duncan Campbell.
Printed and bound in Canada by Transcontinental Printing.

National Library of Canada Cataloguing in Publication Data

Begamudré, Ven, 1956-
The phantom queen

ISBN 1-55050-200-X

I. Title.
PS8553.E342P42 2002   jC813'.54   C2002-910313-4
PZ7.B3882133Ph 2002

10   9   8   7   6   5   4   3   2   1

COTEAU BOOKS   AVAILABLE IN THE US FROM
401-2206 Dewdney Ave.   General Distribution Services
Regina, Saskatchewan   4500 Witmer Industrial Estates
Canada   S4R 1H3   Niagara Falls, NY   14305-1386

The publisher gratefully acknowledges the financial assistance of the Saskatchewan Arts Board, the Canada Council for the Arts, including the Millennium Arts Fund, the Government of Canada through the Book Publishing Industry Development Program (BPIDP), and the City of Regina Arts Commission, for its publishing program.

for David Albahari
for S.D.M. and E.L.M.
also for Shonagh Irvine
and, once again, for Shelley

THE KINGDOM OF MIR

CONTENTS

CAST OF CHARACTERS

IN THE VILLAGE OF DHEREVNIA:
Father Sashenik – *a priest*
Mikhail Illyich – *a wealthy peasant; also called Kulak*
Anna Mikhailovna – *his wife*
Petya Ivanovich – *a baker; also called Boolochnik*
Marya Petrovna – *his wife*
The butcher
The milkmaid
and other villagers

IN THE TOWN OF GOROTH:
Tserkov – *the Bishop of Mir*
Oleg and Olga – *his servants*
Tsar Leo Dherevo – *the King of Mir*
Tsaritsa Elena Lvovna – *the Queen of Mir*
Tsarevna Katrina Lvovna – *the Princess of Mir*
Pavel Virnik – *the collector of bloodwite*
Misha Preestav – *the bailiff*
Nikolai Starik – *the scribe*
Ikar Lvovich – *a prince; later called Ikar Napravo*
Ivan Lvovich – *a prince; later called Ivan Levsha*
Various boyars, or aristocrats, and their lady wives
Other townspeople including a collector
of tolls at a bridge

THROUGHOUT THE KINGDOM OF MIR:
Dhiavol – *the devil known as Satan;*
also called the Evil One

TO BEGIN:

AT THE COURT OF THE

PHANTOM QUEEN

THESE MINSTRELS — THEY ARE NEVER WHAT they seem.

Oh, they begin promisingly enough, but their stories are rarely as compelling as their claims, namely that we will be entertained, enlightened, and enchanted. They also swear that their stories are true. Yet if real life were as fantastic as most of the tales I have heard, why would we need such men to transport us, however briefly, out of our everyday lives? Still, we do need these pretenders, and so they flock to my palace with tales as tangled as beggars' beards. And, like beggars, they drone till I fall asleep. As my daughter likes reminding me, I often drowse through these golden autumn days, even with my grandchildren fussing on my lap. She hints that I should abdicate in her favour, but to drowse like this is the priv-

3

ilege of a monarch who rules a peaceful land. Whose only care is not whether my people live in hunger or in pain – my people do not – but whether I shall hear a tale to match the one I heard on a long-ago and fateful night. The night I removed my chain of office as a chancellor and donned the mantle of a queen.

This is why, of all the men who have woven their tales in this court, I can describe only one. He was old and blind, and yet, the moment he began his tale, everyone – even the hounds, sighing over scraps beneath our tables – fell silent. He began his story like this:

If we measure time by sunrise and sunset,
the waxing and waning of the moon,
the Great Bear's path across the starry dome;
if we measure time by the budding of trees,
the scent of flowers, the sowing of crops and
their harvest;
if we measure time by the drifting of snow,
the melting of ice and the sowing of crops yet
again –
if we measure time in all these natural ways,
my tale must be set long ago.
But if we measure time in the memory of Man,
who recaptures eons through the music of his
words,

then the Mountains of Mir still tower,
and that great river, Mother Reekah, wends
toward the sea.

He stopped to drain his cup of wine, then raised it
for more.

"Just like all the rest," I thought. "He'll drink so
much that his words will slur. He'll forget to gather
the many loose threads of this hoary tale he plans to
weave." In those days I was as impatient as my
daughter is now – not only to replace the old queen
on her throne but also to wed my betrothed –
though my daughter is far more kind than I ever
was. Far less prone to passing judgement, as I did on
this thirsty old man. Yet I could not seem churlish
and so, when the steward looked to me for permis-
sion, I nodded, and he filled the empty cup.

This time the minstrel did not drain it. He
sipped, as if to coax the dust of the road from his
throat, and while he sipped, he looked about as
though he still had eyes.

True, he did have eyes, but they were as useless to
him as his harp would have been had he lacked ears.
His eyelids were as heavy as his step. Wrinkled and
leathery, they covered sunken orbs that moved to
and fro while groping in the dark. The right side of
his face, too, was wrinkled, as one might have

expected of a man who was then older than I am now, but the left side of his face was not wrinkled. Nor was it smooth. Across his cheek, the skin was puckered in waves, while across his temple the skin was as taut as the pulsing head of a drum. There was nothing new in this. As long as we look to fire to heat our halls and cook our food, we must take the bad with the good, and he had at least survived his own battle with fire. It had spared his nose, mouth, and chin, and so his ash grey whiskers were not as patchy as the hair that sprouted from the left side of his scalp.

He was two different men. Or a man with two faces. On the right he was whole – almost perfect despite lines that spoke not of wisdom or adventure but of weariness and age – while on the left he was flawed beyond redemption. I did not find his scars fascinating. I found this half of him – the sinister half – repulsive. Yet this was the man I saw, seated as I was at the head table, each time he looked toward our queen, whose gossamer-curtained throne stood on a dais to my far left.

Now he raised his cup to her. "I have heard," he said, "that you never speak to outsiders. When I asked at the border of your kingdom, 'Who rules here?' I was told, 'The Phantom Queen. She rides among us veiled, lest our gazing upon her face enchants us into forgetfulness. And only those who serve at court may hear her voice.' Blind as I am, I can never see your face, but part that curtain I hear whispering in front of your throne. Speak, so that I may praise your wisdom across the Middle Earth Sea on whose northern shore you rule."

Everyone except the minstrel watched me rise. He faced the head table only when my chain of office clinked. "I speak for Her Majesty," I announced. "I am her chancellor. Any man who hears her voice can never leave this court – as the foreign merchants, our guests, well know." These merchants nodded as if I had spoken some great truth, yet they did so only because they sought favour from me to ply their shoddy wares in our land. "Her Majesty –" I began. Then I paused to search for words as eloquent as his own. " – is like the sun, without whose life-giving rays all creatures must weaken and die." Fine words, yes, that masked my fear of what might befall our land if – no, when – she should leave us.

A few lords, those still jealous of my lofty position, snorted at my use of formal language in order to sound courtly. My beloved, as eager as I to taste the joys of the marriage bed, scowled these men into silence. He was practising to be a prince, although, with our queen as hale as she was aged, he suspected that some time would pass before he could sit in purple robes at my right hand. As for our queen, she did not look at me. She had eyes only for the minstrel, who had none even for himself. How I envied her that regal face. The lines across her brow, the lines fanning outward from her eyes – these spoke of wisdom and adventure. She was always so kind. Never had I seen her eyes flash or heard her voice raised. She treated us like favoured children – no, like brothers and sisters – and when she nodded to acknowledge something that one of us had said, we felt as if she were bowing. As if each of us wore her crown.

"We are willingly her slaves," I told the minstrel. "Would you remain here forever?"

He mocked me with a grin, one made all the more hideous by the half mask of his face. "Lady Chancellor," he said. "Years ago, a certain king offered me his youngest daughter's hand in marriage if I would remain at his court, but a minstrel who chanted all his tales would become as refreshing as an empty wineskin. Besides, I know only one tale, and it takes but a single night to tell. I bind myself to no one." He looked off to his right so that he faced the throne once more. Beneath his eyelids, those useless orbs caressed the curtain as if marvelling at its weave.

The curtain was light to the touch – so fine that

one could have passed the entire cloth through the ring on the queen's right hand – and yet this curtain baffled the light so that she shimmered as if in a rainbowed mist. And that ring. How I coveted it, not for its precious metal but for the jewelled design it bore, the symbol of her reign: a blue-green eagle blazing on a pale orange field. This same eagle rose above the curtain in front of her throne and adorned the banners hung in the hall.

"Part your curtain of silence," he urged our queen. "Speak, even if you then banish me from your kingdom."

"What contrariness is this?" I wondered. "She banishes no one unless he breaks the peace, and how could this rambling old fool leave once he heard her voice?" I did not say these words, but the few words I did speak conveyed my growing annoyance. "Do not provoke me," I warned. Then I sat, and though the merchants nodded at the authority in my voice, my betrothed smiled because he alone knew that I played my part awkwardly – without the casual air of one who is born to wear purple – and in truth I was more annoyed with myself than with the minstrel.

As always, I had spoken boldly, and yet I spoke for a queen about whom I knew little. She had arrived in our kingdom during my father's time. She had been lovely, he said. Simply to gaze on her face had brought peace to a man's troubled mind, and when she spoke – why, a man had not a care in the world. And so our people had crowned her to stop the quarrels that had broken out even as the old king lay dying. On her left hand, she wore a ring that bore his symbol: crossed swords on a red field that spoke of brutish days. I refuse to wear this tarnished ring, but she wore it, my father said, to remind us of the depths to which men can sink. And now, as he had before me, I counselled her and carried out commands without knowing so much as her name.

My loyalty to her was founded not only in the magic of her voice but also in the certainty that I would outlive her. We rarely spoke of this although we both knew that, one day, I would inherit her crown. She had never married, she had not produced heirs, and by now she was too old to bear children even if any man were so bold as to offer himself to her. Yet do not think that I wished her harm. To me, as to others, she truly was the sun with its life-giving rays, and just as I could not bear to look too long at the sun, I could not bear to look too long at her – she enchanted me so. But this was not all. I knew that I had not yet outgrown the impatience of my youth or found the confidence that can ease the headlong passage of a woman through the middle years of her life. I was not yet ready to be queen.

Alas, my daughter understands none of this, and how can I abdicate in her favour until she does understand? This and more.

With a shrug I found impudent, as the minstrel must have known I would, he passed the back of his right hand – the one with which he plucked the strings of his harp – over his lips. They twitched in dismissal of my warning that he not provoke me. Next, he reached down to feel for the staff and the sack that lay beside his chair. These were all he bore besides his blindness and scars and his threadbare clothes: a harp, a staff, a sack.

The harp was a fine instrument made from cherrywood. It was not as ancient as one might have expected to find in such aged hands. I supposed that he had come by it recently, and I wondered how many other harps he had left behind, perhaps trading old harps for new if and when he earned more coins than he spent on keeping together his body and soul. Clearly, he spent little on clothing, and given the threadbare nature of his garments, I wondered how he could present himself like this at courts. Perhaps he rarely entertained at court, or perhaps he was simply vain – one of those itinerant men who like to remind the rest of us how little use they have for worldly goods. Still, if he ever should return – and I know that he will not – I should insist that he accept a new suit of clothes, for it would shame me to see such a raggedy man leave my palace by its front gates.

The staff – ah, yes, the staff. It was nothing special. Like his foreign shoes, it was caked with dust, and I fancied that if it were scrubbed and oiled, it might reveal some record of his travels – symbols, perhaps, of other monarchs he had entertained. But who would have chiselled these symbols, since he had neither eyes to do it for himself nor a companion to do it for him? If anything, this staff was his dearest companion despite its crude design. I say crude because, where one might have expected an artful capping of silver or brass, there was only gnarled wood. I could see that the wood had been jagged once, as if he had twisted it off a tree that had been loath to surrender a living branch of itself. Still, his years of caressing the top had worn it as smooth as any carving rubbed with oil and wax, and so it was artful in its own primitive way.

As for the sack, it was made of leather and its drawstring was filthy with sweat from his hands. I am tempted to say that he could manipulate this thong with such skill that he could not have been truly blind, but to do so would embellish this tale of mine. And I am no minstrel. Much later that night – in the early hours of the following day – I would see him open and close that sack, and he would fumble with the drawstring so much that I would weary of his feeble attempts to appear sufficient unto himself. Impatient for him to be off, now that his own tale was done and he so generously paid.

Having reassured himself that the staff and sack lay beside his chair, he straightened, and the moment he plucked the harp held firmly on his left knee, the courtiers and foreign merchants ceased their murmuring. The hounds fell silent once more, and servants huddling at doorways lowered their flagons of ale. As for the queen, I noticed her stifle a yawn. She looked apologetic at once, for as is the custom in any court, the minstrel addressed his tale to her. Still, it annoyed me that he told his tale as if the rest of us were not even there. As if no one existed except this blind old man and our queen. While the story unfolded, she had eyes only for him and for the ring she twisted on the fourth finger of her right hand – that ring whose jewelled eagle I had kissed on countless occasions of state even as I had longed for the day it would grace my own right hand.

"Your Majesty," he declared. "Lady Chancellor," he added, after a pause that irked me. "My lords, ladies, and merchants and, yes, even you hospitable and courtly servants, I give you a tale for the old to hear and the young to remember."

How much he invented, I cannot guess, but I have commanded his story set down just as I remembered it. As the old queen once declared, no one may change a word of another man's tale unless prepared to make it his own. Unless prepared, especially, for the evil ends to which some men will twist any tale, however much good it was meant to inspire. "We shall always live among such men," she warned — during one of the countless dialogues of my apprenticeship. "Yet this is no reason for good men to hold their tongues or to stop passing on such tales. For a land that does not exist in the imagination of its people," she said, "will not exist for long on a map."

Forgive me, I digress, as I am wont to do — now not because I am enamoured of the sound of my own voice, as I was in earlier times, but because, as my daughter likes reminding me, I am getting on in years and would surely welcome the chance to rid myself of the burden of my crown.

The minstrel's tale, then.

PART ONE:

THE
APPRENTICE,
ONE WHO HAS HEARD

CHAPTER 1:
MONSTER CAVE

FAR NORTH BEYOND THE DANCING GREEN northern lights, a river called the Reekah flowed through the valley of the Kingdom of Mir. People worshipped this river as the bringer of life, and many streams refreshed its pure waters. The Reekah itself began as a stream, one called the Neva, which flowed from a cave beyond a meadow on a mountain called Uroth Gorah. Monster Mountain. The Neva trickled down the meadow, then crashed to the valley at Byelleeye Falls. In winter the falls froze into brooding pillars of ice, while in summer they roared. They flung spray so high that it wet the clouds, and a rainbow danced in this spray. Legend claimed that if two lovers passed hand in hand behind the falls without once losing sight of the rainbow, they would live in peace and enter heaven together.

Not far downstream from the falls, the village of Dherevnia stood on the Reekah's left bank. Dozens of cabins ringed a well, and near them stood bath-houses and barns. Each cabin belonged to a family, but one of the villagers made free with them all. He slept where he fancied, ate where he fancied, and washed if he fancied. His name was Sasha, he was ten, and his parents had died in a fire. The roof of their cabin had collapsed and killed them while they had slept. He had lived thanks only to his dog. It had woken him in time to escape the collapsing roof – but not the flames themselves, which burned his hands and face. Later, the villagers claimed that he did not grow as straight as a sapling should, by which they meant it was natural that he spurned the friend-ship of other children for the friendship of his dog.

This dog was named Sovah, and he had strayed into Dherevnia seven days before the fire. At night, he would curl himself at the foot of Sasha's bed as if to guard him from his own family. The villagers laughed at the scruffy brown dog, whose fur was always matted with pine cones and twigs. The butcher and the milkmaid claimed he had caused the fire himself, though they could not say why. And now, with Sovah's help, Sasha earned his keep by grazing the village goats on Uroth Gorah.

No one bothered him here because they feared the cave from which the Neva flowed. They called this cave Uroth Peshchera – Monster Cave – for it looked like an ogre's head rising from the slope. The Neva was the ogre's blue-green tongue. Stone pillars growing in the back, up from the floor and down from the ceiling, guarded its throat like fangs.

But Sasha was not fool enough to tempt fate. He grazed the goats on the meadow above the falls and sat facing east or west to keep one eye on Uroth Peshchera. When hairs prickled on the back of his neck, he turned quickly, and the cave grinned as if he had caught it about to play a prank or, worse, to roll back its tongue with a tasty boy trapped like a fly.

Long before the sun touched mountaintops in the west, Sasha herded the goats home. Although he believed neither the butcher nor the milkmaid, he did believe the village priest. "If you're still on Uroth Gorah at sunset," Father Sashenik would warn, "Uroth Peshchera will eat you." His voice was always breathless with fear. When he spoke, even to give a blessing, Sasha felt caterpillars crawling down his neck. And, as though the priest himself had willed it, late one afternoon Sasha fell asleep.

The sun glowed more warmly these days than it had before. It was more than a bright spot in a flat winter sky. Bundled in his goatskin coat, Sasha felt drowsy. He awoke to find the sun resting on a snow-capped peak, with a few last rays trickling down the slopes like blood. Then he counted the flock. All the goats grazed nearby on grass that poked through melting snow, but Sovah had vanished.

"Sovah!" Sasha called. He called up and down the meadow and among the trees that bordered it on the east and west. Not a sign. At last he wondered, "What if Sovah chased a hare into the cave and got lost? Who knows how far it goes into the mountain?" He looked at the goats, then at his pipe. A villager had carved it from a willow twig, and its flute-like sound could pierce the roar of the falls.

Clutching the pipe, Sasha decided he could never admit to having fallen asleep. "The villagers will punish me," he thought. "They'll let another boy graze the flock. Even make me help with spring planting. Then I might as well be an ox." Still, he knew that if he set foot in Uroth Peshchera, he might never come out. And yet Sasha knew no one who had lost kinfolk to the cave. What if Father Sashenik had been spinning tales, just as his wife spun wool into yarn for young mothers to knit? But how could a mere boy prove a village priest wrong?

Step by step, Sasha approached the cave. Slanting rays struck the mouth so that its right side glowed while the left side remained dark. He gathered courage with a deep breath and called, "Sovah!"

"So-vah!" the cave yelled back. "So-vah-vah-vah!"

Sasha cringed. But listen. Had Sovah growled just now? Why then did he not appear? Wait, though. What if he had found treasure hidden in the cave? Sasha's eyes gleamed when he thought of the new aprons he could buy for all the women. And the new axes for the men. This would stop the villagers' grumbling about the food he took from their mouths. They thought he did not hear them, but he did. He placed his pipe on the edge of the stream and made to lean his goatherd's crook against the cave's mouth. Then he heard a distant yelp. Not a sharp one of fright or pain but a surprised, howling yelp.

Sasha clutched his crook and entered the cave.

At this very moment, the leading villager of Dherevnia, a man so important that he employed two other men, was muttering over his evening meal. His name was Mikhail Illyich – Mikhail, the son of Illya – but his few friends called him Kulak, which meant a wealthy peasant or one who is tight-fisted. "Where is that boy?" Kulak demanded. "Didn't he say he would sleep here tonight? Does he expect us to call him when his meal is ready?"

Anna Mikhailovna – Anna, the wife of Mikhail – pursed her lips at her husband's lack of charity.

"Oh, very well," he said. He dipped pine branches in a barrel of pitch to make two torches, then lit them from the stove. "Here," he said and handed the smaller of the torches to his son. Leaving their food cooling on the table, pretending annoyance at Anna's whispered prayers for their safe return, father and son set off. When they found the goats bleating on the meadow – bleating for someone to guide them down a slippery path – Kulak told his son, "Take them home. If I'm not back by sunrise, tell Father Sashenik to bring an icon. And all the men."

The boy gladly herded the goats downhill.

Left alone with his pounding heart, Kulak searched among the pines near the meadow. "Stop this foolish game!" he called. "Come back, Sasha, or I'll – !" Kulak's torch cast flickering shadows on tree trunks. The shadows followed him, watched him, and waited to pounce. No frogs croaked. No crickets chirped. Not one bough so much as sighed, for the mountain was holding its breath. Then a bat shot from the cave. The bat shrieked at the moon, but Kulak heard it laughing at him.

At last he approached Uroth Peshchera. Moonlight glinted on its fangs. "Come closer," he imagined the cave saying. "Come in." He followed the stream till he spied Sasha's pipe lying on the bank. "Yes," Kulak heard the cave say, "I ate the boy. No one will miss him. But you – you will be missed."

Kulak's heart sank. Even as he tossed the pipe into the stream, he regretted his rashness, but the pipe twirled beyond his reach and under the melting ice. Angry with himself now, he sat on the bank. "No one in the forest dares enter this place," he thought. "Not even Father Sashenik, and he walks with God. How can a peasant rush in where a priest fears to tread?" And so Kulak's thoughts ran all night while he remained awake; while he remained afraid of falling asleep, alone, on Uroth Gorah.

Shortly before sunrise, Anna Mikhailovna awoke to find her bed cold. Kulak had not returned. She shouted her son awake and told him, "Milk the flock. Then graze the stubborn creatures on another hill. I shall look for your father myself. And for that orphan we must feed."

After her son left, she rose, pulled a woollen skirt over her petticoat, and slipped her feet into shoes of willow bark. No time this morning to untie and comb the sleep from her hair. She coiled her braids on top of her head and knotted a kerchief under her chin. After pulling a shawl about her shoulders, she glanced at a plate near the door. Each evening she put out a morsel of bread for the house sprite, and by morning not a crumb remained. This was good. A house sprite that remained well fed would ensure that her family also remained well fed.

She set off. While she climbed past Byelleeye Falls, she barely noticed the rainbow dancing in the spray. "Only one thing could have happened," she thought. "Mikhail surprised a bear and it dragged him off. O Blessed Virgin," she prayed aloud, "grant my husband protection. And, yes, even that boy." When she reached the top of the falls, she saw that the Virgin had granted one wish, at least.

Kulak sat outside Uroth Peshchera with his chin on his breast. He had wrapped himself in his caftan – his long-sleeved undercoat – tied it closed with his beaded sash, and pulled his felt hat down over his ears. A fire smouldered beside him. He looked up when Anna began to run; when her petticoat swished like wind in the pines. "I couldn't go in after the boy," he groaned. "I still can't."

She sat on the frost-covered bank and leaned against him. They both thought alike: "If only we had been kinder to Sasha. If only we had tried to be father and mother to him." If only this, if only that.

The sun rose above the eastern peaks to light the valley first red, then orange, then yellow-white. Meadowlarks began to sing. Shadows grew longer, then shorter, and the frost began to melt. When the sun reached its highest point in the sky of late winter, the men of Dherevnia appeared. Except for Father Sashenik, all of them wielded axes. He carried an icon of the Blessed Virgin.

"Come home, Mikhail Illyich," Father Sashenik called. "You too, Anna Mikhailovna. The boy has joined his parents."

Kulak shook his head sadly.

Anna glared at the men for believing the worst. "Leave us alone!" she cried. "Why waste your time when there's work to be done? Land readied for sowing, plows repaired. The boy is alive, I tell you!"

"We can't go in the cave or we'll be eaten," Father Sashenik said. He glanced at the mouth and added in his breathless voice, "God's will has been done at last. The boy should not have survived that fire."

The men of Dherevnia nodded.

Anna rose with her tongue sharpened by grief. "Cowards!" she cried. "Even with your axes and icons, you dare not –"

Just then, laughter came from the cave. Eerie laughter that frightened the meadowlarks into silence and froze the blood of men.

Struggling to his feet, Kulak winced at the stiffness in his limbs.

Father Sashenik raised the icon. He made a sign of the cross in the manner of his faith: with his first and second fingers joined as one.

The villagers hefted their axes. Every man waited with his face grim while he feared for his life.

At last, Sasha emerged from behind the fangs, but when Anna opened her arms to him, he remained in the cave. He looked about wildly while tapping his crook on the dirt floor. The wood sounded as if it had turned to iron. An owl perched on his shoulder and blinked at the noon light. Blood matted the tight curls of Sasha's goatskin coat. The ends of his black hair had been singed and yet, strangest of all, the burns on his face and hands had healed. He looked whole once more.

The men glanced at one another for answers to this strange riddle, but even Father Sashenik could offer none.

Kulak told Sasha, "Stop this nonsense. Let's go home."

Sasha frowned. When he said, "I have no home in your village," he sounded grown up, for his words echoed from the cave.

Then Kulak growled in a voice that threatened punishment, "Sasha, you ungrateful – !"

"Don't address me as if I were a child," the boy said. "Call me Nevsky, after this stream. After the Neva, which flows from my true home."

Kulak scratched his beard in wonder.

Anna said, "Very well...Nevsky. We missed you."

He laughed not like a boy but like a man. "No, you didn't," he said. "Your conscience overcame your tight-fistedness. I don't need you any longer. I have my friend, Sovah." When everyone stared at the owl, Sasha-Nevsky said, "Yes, it's him. He doesn't look like a dog any more. He changed during our battle with –"

"Dogs and owls!" the butcher swore. "The boy's gone mad. I warned his parents they were tempting fire when they refused to paint the red rooster above their door!"

"And I warned all of you," another man said. His name was Petya Ivanovich but most people called him Boolochnik, or Baker. "What child could have survived such a fire unless he'd been protected by –" He made the two-fingered sign of the cross in front of his lips, for he had nearly said that most dreaded of names: Dhiavol.

"Now the boy himself has tempted fate," Father Sashenik announced. "I've always said –"

Kulak waved him into silence, then stepped forward.

Sasha-Nevsky raised his crook. "Keep your distance," he warned. "No ordinary man may set foot in Uroth Peshchera. Strangers, above all. Nor on this hill, this mountain. From now on, Uroth Gorah is mine."

"Strangers?" Kulak exclaimed. "You have gone mad!" When he spat in the stream, the spittle eddied under the thinning ice. "Let's go, Anna," he said. "We have our own son to think of. He won't wander off like a madcap when he should be pulling his weight with a plow."

She reached out for Sasha-Nevsky. "What did you see in there?" she cried. "What demon stole your heart?"

"I met countless demons," he said, "but I kept my heart. Go back to your peasant ways of scratching a living from Damp Mother Earth."

"Scratching a living?" Boolochnik demanded. "I burn my fingers baking bread to feed Dherevnia!"

"Foolish boy," Father Sashenik said. "What do you know of peasant ways, you who have never tilled your own land?"

Sasha-Nevsky scowled at the priest. "I learned that knowledge is more important than spending one's life giving birth and burying the dead – till those we bear must bury us, in turn." He threw back his shoulders and planted the crook at his feet. "I also learned that my parents were right to ignore your superstitious ways. Painting red roosters to ward off fire! Leaving bread on plates for house sprites! Don't you see that mice eat the bread?"

"There are no mice in Dherevnia," the butcher

scoffed. "The sprites chase them away."

"Or the mice chase the sprites away," Sasha-Nevsky said. He laughed at his own cleverness.

"Are you so wise now that you can tell your elders what to do?" Kulak asked. "All right then, lord it over your mountain!" Muttering curses, he turned on his heel.

Everyone except Anna followed him toward the falls. "Sasha!" she cried, even as Kulak pulled her away. The last the boy saw of her, she was beating her breast and wailing at the sky.

Feeling weary at last, he lay down in front of the fangs. Memories of dreams swirled in his mind: a passage with no end, a two-headed falcon, grasping hands. Puzzling over these memories, which flickered in the cave like sprites, he fell asleep. He awoke to find dawn breaking and Sovah nibbling on a dead mouse.

"From Dherevnia, of course," Sovah said. "You've slept for three days. I've been watching them. The priest convinced Kulak that his house had been cursed." When Sasha-Nevsky laughed, Sovah said, "There's little humour in the ignorance of others. Kulak loaded his belongings onto a cart. All their lives, the ancestors of Mikhail Illyich have lived in the forest. He thinks that the steppe is a desert stretching to the sea, but he has led his family to the gorge in the south. To the village of Konyets. He hopes that the forest will grow around his cabin to erase the villagers' memory of you. His wish is coming true. The trees are swallowing his house just as they swallowed the charred timbers of your own. Soon the villagers will no longer remember you as you were, just as you will no longer remember your parents."

The boy once named Sasha, the boy now called Nevsky, did not hear this last. When he rose and slapped dust from his coat, bloodied curls of goathair fell away to leave smooth brown hide. "There's little to be reaped by dreaming," he said. "To work!"

Wielding his crook like an axe, he felled a tall pine and fashioned its wood into boards. Sovah drilled dovetails into their edges with his beak, and from these boards Nevsky made a door. Then he built a fire in the mouth of Uroth Peshchera. He stoked the flames until the cave roared and the Neva sizzled. Using his crook as a hammer now, and a boulder as an anvil, he smelted iron to fashion hinges, a latch, and a key. All this took a single morning. After setting the door behind the fangs, he crowed, "Now no one but us may enter that other world."

"Is this the knowledgeable boy speaking," Sovah asked, "or the childish goatherd?"

"It's a wise man speaking," Nevsky said. He began damping the fire.

"No," Sovah warned. He flew from the cave and called back, "You're still only a boy. Your journey into manhood is about to begin."

CHAPTER 2:
THE ROAD TO GOROTH

TWICE DURING THE EARLY AFTERNOON, Nevsky ran along the Neva to the top of the falls to see if anyone might be bold enough to climb his mountain. Twice he turned back and sat in the cave, where he listened to voices whispering beyond the door.

The third time he ran to the top of the falls, he looked out over the Kingdom of Mir.

The Reekah flowed south for many miles through forests and then orchards. Next, it flowed between two vast stretches of steppe, which would soon be planted with barley and oats, rye and wheat. In winter the Reekah froze solid and still like Byelleeye Falls, but in summer nothing could stop the river's course. Not even the town of Goroth.

The town stood on an island shaped like a

teardrop with its rounded end facing north. Two bridges arced from the island to the east and west like the wings of a giant bird. North of the island, the forests and orchards came to an end; south of the island, the steppes began. On either side of the island, the Reekah gurgled through swamps. Vegetable gardens would soon be planted here to feed the entire town. In spring the Reekah flooded these gardens and nourished the rich black soil. In summer it watered rows of carrots, turnips, and beets.

On the narrowing end of the island, south of the vast town square, lived the tsar in his palace. North of the square lived the bishop in his cathedral and the monks in their House of Song. Craftsmen and merchants lived in the rest of Goroth. Unlike the peasants of Mir, who made their homes in the forest or on the steppes, the people of Goroth rarely looked up from their work to admire the river. They claimed they had little time for rest.

Once the Reekah crept past the town, its waters flowed with ease. The river gathered strength while nourishing the fields of the steppes. After entering a gorge near the village of Konyets, the Reekah raced for the sea.

From the far, northern edge of the kingdom, Nevsky watched the sun glinting off the cathedral bell tower. He knew that this was a sign – a sign that his journey must begin – and so he said, "Let's go to Goroth."

"Who?" Sovah asked.

"Us."

"How?"

"I on foot and you on the wing. We should be there by sunset." With Sovah perched on his shoulder, Nevsky slid down a path along the left side of Byelleeye Falls. The late winter sun had melted the snow and made the path slippery, so he used his crook to keep his footing. Crocuses poked their shoots above ground to greet the sun, to urge it to climb higher and grow warm. A robin tugged at an earthworm. A groundhog popped out of its burrow to watch the battle and chattered while Nevsky passed. Near the bottom, he began sliding downhill.

Sovah cried, "Look out," and flew from Nevsky's shoulder.

After skidding to a halt, Nevsky tumbled into a puddle. He rose, laughing, to offer Sovah a muddied shoulder. But Sovah flew on to Dherevnia.

When Nevsky reached the village, he stopped to drink at the well and searched for familiar sights. On a knoll behind a mill stood Father Sashenik's church. The villagers had built it from the very trees they had cleared from the knoll. Women working in their cabins watched Nevsky and whispered about him to their daughters. Word was spreading through the forest about the strange boy who slept in Uroth Peshchera. People called him Dhurak, or Fool, for as Sovah had said they would, they had forgotten Sasha the goatherd. When he smiled at the women and girls, the girls smiled back but the women did not.

"How strange," he thought. "They do the same thing day in, day out. I can do what I want. If only I could live among such people, yet not be dulled by their ordinary ways!" A knot of children too young to work watched him from the other side of the well. He wished that one of them might approach him, but when none did, he told himself, "I don't need their friendship."

Before long, the smell of fresh bread made his nostrils twitch. His stomach began to growl, then twist itself with hunger. He was tired of eating roots. He followed the smell to a large cabin on the edge of Dherevnia. The walls were carved with animals and birds, with a red rooster painted above the door. He entered without knocking. Unlike the clear chill of the open air, the cabin felt hot and close, for the doors of a huge oven stood open. Boolochnik was removing loaves with their crust still soft.

The finest bread in the forest came from this cabin. Some people said that his skill made the dough rise just so and no more. Others claimed that the secret lay in his wife's touch; that Marya Petrovna knew which seeds or herbs to press onto which loaf to bring its taste alive. She was sitting in a corner and grinding sage.

Nevsky addressed her as Young Mother when he greeted her, for she was great with child.

At this, Boolochnik asked, "You want some bread, I suppose?" He glared at Sovah, whose feathers remained unruffled.

"Oh, yes," Nevsky said. "I'm hungry."

Scowling at the mud Nevsky had tracked inside, Boolochnik asked, "Am I to feed every beggar whose stomach follows his nose to my door?"

Marya brushed flakes of sage off a pestle into a mortar, then licked her fingers and dried them on her apron. "Can't you see he's no beggar?" she said. "I told you about Dhurak. I heard of him from the butcher's wife. The priest's wife, as well. There's honour in giving holy fools bread. Father Sashenik says so."

"We give him bread, too," Boolochnik scoffed. "Does he call himself a holy fool?" The baker set the warm loaves on a bench to cool. When Nevsky bent over them, he nearly touched one with the tip of his tongue. Boolochnik shooed him away. "Look here," he said. "I'll give you one of these small loaves if you tell me whether Marya bears a boy or a girl." He winked at her before adding, "Wheat bread for a boy, Dhurak. Rye for a girl."

Nevsky shrugged at the feeble jest. "Of course I like wheat," he said, "but you must give me rye. Marya Petrovna will give birth to a girl. And you, Petya Ivanovich, will cast her to the birds. As you do with loaves that are burnt."

Crying, "Never," Boolochnik raised a fist. He drew back when Sovah tried to peck flour off his knuckles. "For that you get nothing," he snarled. "Go! Leave honest people to their work. And who gave you leave to address me with such familiarity?"

Nevsky backed out of the cabin. He bowed to Marya to show that he held her blameless, then turned and ran from the village. Only after entering the forest once more did he slow to a walk. "What ails that baker?" he asked Sovah.

"He wanted you to humour him," Sovah said. "Not frighten him with the truth."

Nevsky shrugged and continued toward Goroth. There were no berries on bushes or fruit on trees, and his stomach growled so loudly that it scared off the mice Sovah tried to catch. True, the ice covering the Reekah was so thin that Nevsky could see gurgling water, but it was still too early to expect Damp Mother Earth to feed him. There was also no one to offer him food because no one else passed. In summer, carts could rumble easily over the dry road; in winter, sleighs could skim over packed snow or on ice covering the river. But now in late winter, as in early spring, wheels and runners sank in the mud.

Nevsky reached Goroth at sunset, even as one last ray touched the gold cross atop the cathedral. With his eyes on the glow, he approached the east bridge, and here a loud voice startled him with, "Well?"

The voice belonged to a stout man who held a tin box. "Are you going to cross or not?" he asked. "Pay up if you're using the bridge." He shook the box under Nevsky's nose, and a single coin rattled against the tin. "Best you pay," the man said. "It'll save you from a dunking. No one uses the bridge during winter, but now misers try to cross the ice and pay with a cold bath. I should sell blankets, I should."

Pointing at the cathedral, Nevsky said, "That's all the gold I have."

The toll collector looked up at the glowing cross. He muttered, "All day, I stand here collecting coins. Spring, summer, and fall I stand here and yet not once have I noticed this glow."

He watched till the glow faded. When he finally looked about, Nevsky waved at him from the far end of the bridge. The toll collector laughed and waved back. He rattled his box and laughed once more.

Nevsky made for the cathedral.

What other kingdom on Earth could boast of such a monument to God and Man? Built of the finest oak, the cathedral had an eight-sided tower at each of its four corners. Each tower rose into a dome shaped like an onion – a reddish-gold coppery dome. In the midst of these towers rose a bell tower topped by a huge central dome, also sheathed in copper. On it stood the cross.

Nevsky entered by the main doors and hid behind a pillar. The bishop had finished celebrating the evening Mass, and worshippers yawned while they hurried out. Alone now except for Sovah, Nevsky wandered through the cathedral, and more than once he shook his head in awe.

On the rounded ceiling beneath the bell tower was a portrait of Christ with His arms spread. His left hand pointed east. Here, men and women were roasted on spits and devoured by wolves only to be coughed up whole and roasted once more. His right hand pointed west, where peasants and nobles danced in a heavenly field. Paintings covered the walls, as well – paintings in which saints gave their clothes to beggars or healed the sick.

Lovelier than these paintings were the mosaics. Made of hundreds of tiles in blue and green, yellow and red, they showed fantastic animals like horses with the heads of men, women with the tails of fish. And the fragrance! Even the scent of the sweetest wood paled beside the incense burning at every pillar, the beeswax melting on golden sticks.

The cathedral felt so peaceful that Nevsky could hear the wax drip, drip. He had dreamt of such a place once, in his cave, yet now he scarcely knew if he was in heaven or on Earth.

As quietly as the toll collector had approached, the bishop re-entered from a side door. Nevsky noticed him only when Sovah flew off his shoulder to land on the back of a pew.

Bishop Tserkov wore a simple black robe and a high black hat. On his breast dangled a cross. It shone amidst the hairs of his white beard, which fell to his waist. Some people claimed he was a hundred years old. How else, they asked, could he have brought the Word of God to a land with mountains as high as those that surrounded Mir? There was some truth to this. He had, indeed, brought the words of his God to the kingdom, but he could not remember them all – he was that old. He stopped and placed his hands on Nevsky's head.

"Greetings, my son," Tserkov declared. "People always leave so quickly, afraid that their soup will grow cold. Why do you stay?"

"I didn't attend your Mass," Nevsky replied. "I

don't need to be in a church or a cathedral to speak with God."

"And do you speak with Him often?"

"Mostly, I think, He speaks to me."

Fingering his beard now, Tserkov looked more closely at Nevsky and saw a boy in a patched linen shirt belted over torn trousers. Dust covered his coat. Mud caked his boots so thickly that even someone as wise as a bishop could not guess their colour. "Poor boy," he thought. "No doubt an orphan from the countryside. What mother would let her son visit our town looking so bedraggled? Loneliness has driven him mad." Tserkov gestured to the paintings and mosaics. "Do you understand the stories they tell?" he asked.

"Some of them," Nevsky replied.

"Who taught you?"

"I teach myself."

"Does this mean you can read?"

"I don't know. I've never tried. Just now, I'd rather eat than read."

"Let's eat, then."

"Come, Sovah," Nevsky said.

The owl returned to Nevsky's shoulder. When the bishop raised a hand in greeting, Sovah winked, and Tserkov realized he had seen the owl before – countless times – but where? Puzzling over this, he led

Nevsky toward the royal doors that separated the nave, where worshippers sat, from the sanctuary, which contained the altar. Above the royal doors hung row upon row of icons glinting candlelight from their gold leaf. After turning to the right and skirting the royal doors, Tserkov opened a plain wooden one. It led to the southeast tower, one of the two that overlooked the square.

A man and a woman hurried from a kitchen into the main room. They were short and stocky like the peasants of the forest, not tall and thin like the people of Goroth.

"This is Oleg," Tserkov said. "He puts the candles out after Mass. And this is his wife, Olga. She bakes the wafers that stand for –"

"The Body of Christ," Nevsky said.

Laughing, Tserkov declared, "And you say you don't attend Mass?" He told his servants, "My new friend is – ?"

Nevsky announced his name.

"And you are from which village?"

"I live at the source of the Neva."

"I see," Tserkov said, though there was much that he did not yet see. "As for the owl," he announced, "I heard him called Sovah. Set another place, Oleg, if you please. More bread, Olga, if you please."

The servants obeyed, then watched silently from

the kitchen while their master entertained his strange guest.

Nevsky ate two servings – the first quickly to ease his hunger, the second more slowly to relish the simple food: beef and boiled turnips. Sovah took a chunk of bread and perched on a beam above the table. Crumbs fell while he pecked out and swallowed the poppy seeds. When Nevsky at last brushed the crumbs from his hair, they reminded him of Boolochnik, and so he recounted his passage through Dherevnia.

"How did you guess that the mother will bear a girl?" Tserkov asked. He shook his head when Olga offered to refill his plate.

Nevsky had just taken a large bite of bread and honey. After he chewed and swallowed, he licked the honey off his fingers. He wiped them on his shirt instead of on a square of linen folded next to his plate. At last he replied, "I don't guess. I know."

"And how do you know so much, my son?"

"I hear voices."

"In this home you call Uroth Peshchera?"

"They're loudest in my home, yes, but I heard them in Dherevnia, too. In the baker's cabin. And here they told me the stories in the paintings and mosaics."

"I see," the bishop said again.

After Nevsky and Tserkov finished eating, they sat in front of a fireplace while Oleg cleared the table. Tserkov drank mead, brewed by the monks out of honey and water. After each sip, he sprinkled pepper on the mead because he found it too sweet now, in his old age. Nevsky drank kvass, an ale made from rye – a sour brew more suited to a man's taste than a boy's. Birch logs burned brightly. They crackled and spat. He saw images in the flames: two hands, a burning bridge, a blazing white dove. Yet he felt too tired to puzzle over their meaning. Soon he fell asleep and dreamt of a copper dome like the cathedral's central dome, but the dome of his dream rose so high that it snagged the clouds on its cross. So high that it filled the very dome of the sky and pressed the stars through the fabric of night – into the sky of another world.

When Tserkov called for Oleg, he came with a candle on a copper stick.

The bishop pointed at Nevsky, who lay curled in a chair with his empty goblet in his lap. "He talks like a man," Tserkov said. "He even tries to drink like a man, and yet he sleeps like a child. Take him to my room." He lit the way up winding stairs while Oleg carried Nevsky. They tucked him into the bishop's soft bed and closed its curtains against the chill.

After returning to the main room, Tserkov bade

Oleg good night. Then the bishop saw Nevsky's crook leaning next to the fireplace. The crook intrigued him because when he examined it closely, he found symbols carved in the ashwood. There were common ones like stars, moons, and lightning bolts. There were others less common, and far more worrying, like scorpions. When he reached out to turn it, Sovah opened his eyes.

Perched on the mantel, he had been pretending to sleep. "Who?" he demanded.

To Tserkov, it sounded like, "Doom."

He straightened and said, "You're right. I don't like people touching my crozier. They smudge the gold."

He settled on his daybed and pulled a woollen blanket up to his chin. He arranged his beard outside the blanket so the night air would keep it soft. Even though he could not spend the night in his own bed, he felt content because God had granted him his fondest wish. Or so he hoped.

The priests of Tserkov's faith could marry and could father children, but priests could not become bishops. Only monks could become bishops, and yet monks could not marry. Even as a boy, Tserkov had dreamt of wearing gold robes on holy days, of celebrating Mass not in a church but in a cathedral, and so he had become a monk. He had tried to forget that he could never share his bed with a wife or fulfill his dreams of fatherhood. Perhaps now, at last, God had sent him, if not a wife, then a child of sorts.

He fell asleep with a smile on his crinkled lips.

Sovah closed his all-seeing eyes.

The next morning, before the slanting rays of the rising sun touched the cross on the cathedral, a voice woke Nevsky. It whispered a single word: "Search."

He crept downstairs while rubbing his eyes. The embers in the hearth had grown cold, and Tserkov lay fast asleep. Sovah was already aloft, Nevsky knew. Seeing his crook, he straightened his left arm. The crook twitched as if shaking off sleep, then flew to his hand. He allowed it to lead him out of the southeast tower, past the royal doors, and into the northwest tower.

Even as a heavy door swung open before him, he knew he had discovered a treasure, at last — one that was worthless to some yet priceless to others. He entered a library that contained nearly a hundred books. One of them lay open on a reading stand, near the window, and he saw that the book was called *The Virgin Mary's Journey Through the Inferno.* Neat round script covered the parchment, and many pages contained illuminated scenes. Soon the sky outside lightened, and a bluebird sang in a bush. Sovah returned, perched on

Nevsky's shoulder, and also read.

By the time Tserkov found them, they had read most of a second book. This one had been written in Greek.

"So here you are," he exclaimed. "Oleg searched for you in the kitchen, but it seems you weren't hungry for food." The bishop stood at the window, which overlooked the monks' House of Song. "What are you reading?" he asked.

Nevsky read aloud: "'In the wild forest, where the axe went, the plow followed, then the icon. The houses of animals became the houses of men.' That must be how villages like Dherevnia began."

Tserkov nodded. Half to Nevsky, half to himself, he muttered while caressing other books. "It's often cold in here, but I forget this the moment I open any one of these old friends. Over the years, I've dictated everything I know and much I've forgotten. The monks wrote my words with care. Then they illuminated the capital letters with tincture and leaf. A book such as this takes one of my brothers an entire year to write and another year to illuminate. Now you can read them, too. The tsar reads them sometimes but understands little. He remembers the words only long enough to impress his courtiers. Stay as long as you want, my son. From today, Oleg will leave the door unlocked." Tserkov frowned at

Nevsky. "How did you get in? Oh, never mind. I see that you come and go as you wish."

During the weeks that followed Nevsky's first visit to Goroth — while winter melted into spring — he did come and go as he wished. He spent one week in his cave and the next in the cathedral. As an orphan protected by the church, he never had to pay for crossing the bridge, but the toll collector looked forward to seeing him.

Each time Nevsky crossed onto the island, he pointed out something that the toll collector had seen but never truly noticed: blackbirds teetering on rushes, shadows of carp in the river, swallow nests among the beams. A new light shone from his eyes. He acted as if he had spent all his years before this one deaf and blind, and yet people noticed that he no longer sounded as jolly as he once had.

Tserkov also looked forward to seeing Nevsky, but soon the bishop found himself disappointed with the boy. Tserkov wanted to discuss the arts of men, their beliefs and their fears, but Nevsky spoke about the histories of people unknown to Tserkov — unknown because they had yet to walk the earth. He also disappointed the bishop by never taking part in Mass. Nevsky did enjoy watching it. He learned the stories behind every icon, painting, and mosaic. He inhaled the aromas of beeswax and incense. Best of all, he shivered with joy when the deep-voiced monks chanted separate melodies that blended in the slanting pillars of sunlight. All the sights and smells and sounds pointed the way to God, yet Nevsky walked his own road – to where, Tserkov could not guess.

One evening, Sovah upset a dish of sweetmeats in the library. When Nevsky bent to pick them up, a necklace of bear's teeth slipped out from behind the high collar of his linen shirt. On the necklace dangled the key to the door in Uroth Peshchera. After he tucked the necklace out of sight, he looked up to find Tserkov staring at him.

"Where did you get that?" the bishop demanded. "Only a warrior who has killed a bear may wear its teeth."

"A she-bear named Medvyedeetsa gave them to me," Nevsky replied. "After Sovah found honey for her cubs. These were the teeth of her father, who died peacefully, not at the hand of some warrior aching to prove his skill."

"I don't know if you should wear such a necklace in Goroth," Tserkov said. "People might think you stole it."

Nevsky snapped a sweetmeat in two. "Let them think what they want," he said. "I live only for myself and Sovah, not for others. They call me

Dhurak. They call me Fool. They look so pleased with themselves when they give me bread because they care more about their souls than they do for my body. You're the only one who truly cares." He ate half the sweetmeat and gave the other half to Sovah.

Tserkov turned to hide his dismay. "I shouldn't judge you so harshly," he thought. "Yet sometimes I think you take pleasure in irking those who wish to be kind. You know so much, but not the most important thing of all: how to love. How can you learn this when you live like a hermit and care only for animals and books? A dozen times you've said, 'Knowledge is more important than love.' Oh, my son, until you discover that this is not so, you'll remain an apprentice, one who has heard. You'll never become a master, one who has seen. But who can teach you this lesson? And when will it begin?"

Sovah repeated, "Who?"

To Tserkov, it sounded like, "Soon."

CHAPTER 3:
LEO THE LUCKLESS

BLESSED IS THE KING WHO RULES A PEACEFUL kingdom; yet cursed is the king who forgets to count his blessings every day of his reign. Such a man was Tsar Leo Dherevo, Leo the Tree. By his twenty-first birthday, he had been gored by a stag, trampled by an elk, and bitten by a wolf. He had killed a bear, shot countless deer, and caught and tamed a dozen wild horses. But all bones grow brittle, and once his hair began to grey, Leo grew tired of the hunt. He surrounded himself with his warriors in the Palace of Goroth. He had little need of them, for no one meant him harm, so they served only to roar with laughter at tales of his carefree youth. His boyars – the aristocrats – might as well have lived in the palace, too. They owned manors in the countryside and winter houses in town but passed as much time at court as they did at home. Leo took no notice of the food and drink these hangers-on consumed, for he spent far more time with them than he did with his own family.

He kept his wife, Elena, and their seven daughters out of sight. All day, they sat in the palace tower and made lace as pale and delicate as their skin – a yard of lace for every tear of boredom filling eyes that rarely saw the sun. The kingdom they knew was a land of rooftops, treetops, and steppes tinted brown by the mica panes of the tower windows. It was not that Leo did not love his wife and daughters. It was just that seeing them reminded him he had no sons.

He tried every remedy known to man. Each year, magicians and physicians came to the palace on the first day of spring, which also marked the beginning of the holy days called Easter. On this day, the sun triumphed in its battle with frost, and the last shards of ice floated down the Reekah. The magicians gave Elena powders and herbs. The physicians gave Leo advice. Nothing helped. He hung his head when he allowed himself to be alone, for he thought that his people laughed at him. He was wrong. They called him Leo the Luckless not because he had no sons but because he could not be content.

Tserkov celebrated the start of Easter with a special noon Mass. As always, Nevsky watched from the back of the cathedral, then joined the bishop at his table. They had just broken bread when someone knocked loudly on the outer door.

"What's this?" Tserkov demanded.

Oleg ran to see who would dare disturb the bishop at his midday meal. Moments later, he ushered in a tall young man with his bearskin coat unbuttoned. He kept tugging at his flaxen beard or at the golden chain about his neck. Despite such signs, only Nevsky saw how troubled the young man looked.

"Christ is risen!" Tserkov said in the age-old greeting of Easter.

The young man quickly gave the response: "In truth, risen!"

Tserkov introduced Nevsky and Sovah. Then the bishop said, "My son, this is Lord Pavel Virnik. He —"

"I know," Nevsky said. He nodded at the golden dagger dangling from the golden chain. "Lord Virnik collects the bloodwite, the fine that people must pay the tsar if they kill someone. He is also the youngest boyar in Mir."

"And prefers to be called by his given name," Tserkov added.

"Enough," Pavel said. "You'd best come at once, or I'll have to collect from Leo himself."

Tserkov exclaimed, "What? Oleg, my coat!"

Nevsky snatched his crook from its place near the fire. He waited at the door to lend Tserkov one shoulder, and Sovah perched on the other. Then they followed Pavel outside and across the town square.

Above each of the palace's iron gates rose half of a two-headed falcon with one beak pointing east and the other pointing west. Only when the gates were closed did the falcon appear whole. Nevsky was about to remark on this when the guard at the gates asked, "Who's this ragamuffin with his silly bird?"

Pavel snapped, "Can't you see? He's the bishop's walking stick. The owl is the bishop's eyes. Out of our way!"

The guard snorted at the young boyar but did step aside.

On they went, and despite the haste Nevsky admired his surroundings. Every inch of the corridor walls had been carved with scenes from peasant life. Here, men built a cabin in the forest; there, women drew water from a well; and, farther along, boys and girls danced in fields of wheat that arced in the wind. Torches blazed in brackets, and every latch was gold.

At last, Pavel stopped at double doors – above which rose yet another two-headed falcon. He threw them open, then stepped aside to let Tserkov enter first. After following the men, Nevsky skipped behind a wooden pillar. He knew he did not belong in such a place, and he had no wish to meet any more guards puffed with disdain, so he peeked carefully around the pillar.

Tsar Leo was standing in front of the throne and pounding clenched fists on his thighs. On either side of the room stood his foremen, his six eldest boyars. Other boyars and his many warriors lined both sides of the long room. As a sign of their loyalty, boyars wore neck chains, and warriors bore neck rings. When Pavel had thrown open the doors, the warriors had reached for their weapons, and even now they could not stand at ease.

None of this surprised Nevsky, but he frowned at the man who knelt on the inlaid floor in front of the throne. The man's wrists were tied behind his back.

"What goes on here?" Tserkov demanded. He was approaching the tsar slowly, for he walked with no support.

"Ah," Leo said, "the bishop leaves his cathedral. For once."

Ignoring the warriors' laughter, Tserkov stopped only when he reached the plain but massive throne. Above it rose a golden two-headed falcon with its wings spread. It symbolized the tsar's duty to protect his people – a duty that, Nevsky saw, Leo seemed to have forgotten. Speaking with more respect than before, Tserkov asked, "What do you mean to do, sire?"

"This so-called physician," Leo said, pointing at the kneeling man, "claims I can't have any more children. I'll imprison him for lying. I'll confiscate his property."

"You won't!" Tserkov touched the man's head and the man looked up. "He's under my protection, just like my servants and those who till church land." The bishop pointed past the ceiling toward the sky. "A physician's property belongs to me or, if not to me, then to —"

"Oh, very well," Leo grunted, "but the man must be punished. Have his tongue torn out. Once I couldn't father sons, you see. Now this charlatan says I can't father children at all. He says I've grown too old! It's Elena who's old, not I. It's her fault, not mine. This yearly farce must end. No more physicians concocting foul potions! No more magicians rolling their eyes like idiots! I'm taking more wives, a dozen if I must. One of them will bear me a son."

Tserkov slapped his wrinkled cheeks in horror. "You can't," he gasped. "You'll become like your grandfather before I christened him. Just another pagan —"

"Bah!" Leo kicked at the bearskin rug beneath his feet.

Tserkov pointed at the throne. "Listen to me, Leo Dherevo. You owe me your very crown. Your grandfather had many sons by many wives. His grandsons, your foremen, are here even now. But you're the king. Why? Because after I christened your grandfather, he chose his first wife, your grandmother, as tsaritsa. As queen. Even if you've forgotten this, surely your scribe remembers?"

This scribe, a man named Nikolai Starik, nodded reluctantly. Perched on a stool near the throne, he made notes on parchment that covered a slab of wood. When he glanced up, he looked like a bird of prey, and this was why boyars called him a vulture, though never to his face. Only Tserkov did not fear him. Many a boyar had drained many a cup while arguing about which of them was the elder – the bishop or the scribe. Some even claimed that they were brothers; that they had quarrelled after having arrived in Mir from a distant land. True, they had come from afar, long before the Mountains of Mir had grown impassable, but the two men hailed from different lands: Tserkov's sunny and warm, Starik's as gloomy as it was cold.

The bishop again touched the physician's head and this time asked, "Sire?"

Leo flicked his hand. "Oh, very well," he said. "Let him keep his tongue, but get him out of my sight!"

Pavel helped the physician to his feet, cut his bonds, and led him from the room while he chafed at his wrists. A guard closed the doors Pavel had thrown open.

Still unnoticed by everyone, Nevsky crept from pillar to pillar till he neared the throne. Leo reminded him of a sulky bear. He glowered at his courtiers as though searching for someone else to fault. He twirled the ends of his drooping moustache, then paced while everyone remained silent. Snatching off his cap and throwing it down, he revealed that he was bald except for a lock of reddish grey hair. This lock hung down the left side of his head as a sign of royal birth, but he would have looked regal even in a peasant's sarafan.

Not that he wore such clothes. He wore a caftan of purple whose tight sleeves ended in gold cuffs. He wore purple trousers tucked into high green boots. Rubies studded his belt. Over the caftan and trousers, he wore a dark blue sleeveless robe. The wings of a two-headed ruby falcon held the robe closed at his breast. And the gold hem of his robe was so stiff that it rustled while he paced.

Tired of pacing, he snatched up his cap and slapped off hairs from the bearskin rug. He flung himself onto his throne and threw one leg over a carved arm. His leg dangled like a broken branch creaking in the wind, and his boot heel thudded on wood. He turned his sable cap inside out to look at its gold lining. Then he glowered at his courtiers again. No one had dared speak while he'd stormed, and now he grew sullen because no one broke the silence. He stared at a stag's head mounted on the wall.

"Bishop," he said at last, "why is God punishing me? What evil have I ever done or commanded?" He looked at Tserkov and laughed. "You know I've never had a man's tongue torn out. His hair, perhaps, but never his tongue."

Tserkov said nothing.

When Nevsky left the safety of one last pillar, a warrior pointed him out to the bailiff, a boyar named Misha Preestav. He was about to signal another warrior when Nevsky tugged at Tserkov's robes.

"Perhaps he isn't," Nevsky said.

Leo sat up and asked, "What?"

Nevsky told the tsar, "Perhaps God isn't punishing Your Majesty. Perhaps it's time for the crown to go to a woman."

"Who let this peasant in?" Leo shouted. "Is every guard asleep?"

Preestav cringed. He ran forward to snatch Nevsky's arm, then looked about for someone to blame. "He must have slipped in during the commotion," the bailiff said. "Come along, you!"

Tserkov brushed at the golden keys dangling

from Preestav's golden chain. "Nevsky is also under my protection," the bishop said.

"Are you a tree," Leo asked, "that every good-for-nothing seeks shelter under your branches? I thought I was the tree here!"

The courtiers laughed.

When Leo waved his hand, Preestav stepped aside. Still, he kept one eye on Nevsky and the other on Sovah, who remained on Nevsky's shoulder.

"Nevsky, Nevsky," Leo muttered. He asked Starik, "Isn't there a village called Neva near the gorge?"

"No, sire," the scribe said. "The Neva is a stream in the north. You're thinking of a village called Konyets in the south. I've heard of this Dhurak. He lives in a cave and —" Starik fell silent because Leo was no longer listening.

He was toying with a ruby that dangled from his right ear. A smile almost brightened his face while he looked at Nevsky from head to foot. The boy looked funnier than the motley buffoons who visited Goroth during festivals, and yet Leo frowned because Nevsky seemed to look right through him.

"All the wise men in Mir have failed me," Leo said. "Perhaps I'll seek the counsel of a fool." He gestured for Nevsky to approach.

"Kneel before the tsar," Preestav commanded.

"If this is a church," Nevsky said, "where is the altar?"

The courtiers gasped. No one except Tserkov and Starik dared to speak like that in court.

Scowling at the bailiff, Leo asked, "Will pomp bring me a son? Leave him! Well, Nevsky-Dhurak, why does God ignore my wishes?"

"What is it you wish for?" Nevsky said.

Leo replied as if reciting a prayer he knew by heart: "That my people live in peace, that they never hunger or thirst, and that I leave them a prince to crown."

"Aren't peace and prosperity enough?" Nevsky asked. "If God gave you everything, you might stop believing in Him."

The boyars muttered among themselves. Preestav muttered the loudest.

"Take care, my son," Tserkov whispered. "Scribes write only what tsars wish to remember, but Starik never forgets such words."

Nevsky raised his voice above the muttering. "Your Majesty is being selfish," he said. "Aren't you content knowing that your subjects live so well? There are kingdoms in which people grow fat on their neighbours' flesh and drunk on their neighbours' blood. Kingdoms in which even petty chieftains leave no heirs." He pointed at a knot of warriors under the stuffed head of a doe. "Show your-self," he called.

At this, a young woman of thirteen elbowed her way through the warriors. She wore a red dress with loose sleeves gathered at her wrists. About her waist she had knotted a wide gold sash, and onto her hair she had pinned a lace kerchief. Her squirrel's fur slippers made no sound while she approached. Had she not walked with her head held high, she might have been a peasant, for she resembled Leo too closely to be beautiful. Yet Nevsky saw that God had planted the seeds of wisdom in her eyes. They were eyes as bright as Pavel's, who now had eyes only for her.

Bowing to the young woman, Nevsky announced, "Tsarevna Katrina Lvovna. Daughter of Leo, Princess of Mir."

"Princess or not," Leo shouted, "no woman may enter my throne room! What are you doing in the halls of men?"

When she tossed her head, torchlight glinted from her red hair. "Learning to be tsaritsa," she declared. "Learning to be a queen."

For the first time that day, Leo laughed with true mirth. Soon, though, he slapped the arm of his throne. "You could never rule Mir," he scoffed. "My crown is too large for your head. My axe is too heavy for you to lift, let alone swing. And my cloak would make you look like a dwarf. Imagine," he told his court, "a puny girl shrouded in purple gazing down from this throne like a child from a painted wooden horse!"

When the courtiers laughed, Nevsky said, "These are only ceremonial trappings. Is a kingdom ruled by pomp?"

Preestav snickered until the tsar silenced him with a glare. "How often do you sneak in here?" Leo asked Katrina.

"As often as I please," she replied. "My mother and sisters may not mind being cooped in the tower like pigeons. They may not mind listening to their ladies tell the same old tales and sing the same old songs. But I'm not my mother or my sisters. I won't learn how to make laws by making lace."

"Wha-at!" Dumbfounded, Leo said, "Starik, tell my mad daughter — and this mad country fool — what is written."

Starik closed his eyes while searching for the exact words. Then, with his eyes still shut, he chanted, "Before any woman can wear our tsar's crown, the Reekah must dry up and the mountains fall down."

"And there's precious little chance of that!" Leo said. He smiled his thanks to Starik, who glared haughtily at Tserkov.

"Sire," the bishop said, "God in His wisdom sent

you Katrina. Each time you asked for a son, He sent another daughter. He must have meant Tsarevna Katrina to become queen. He may work in mysterious ways, but He drops the rain or the snow because He wants it to rain or snow. He does not drop hints."

Slouching on his throne, Leo pouted like a child. "Rulers of other kingdoms would laugh at my memory if the crown passed to her," he said. "If they knew. God willing, the mountains would grow even higher if she were crowned. Never! My duty to the dead must be as strong as my duty to the living. No woman has ever ruled Mir!" While he'd spoken, his voice had softened till he'd sounded like an old man blubbering of aches and pains. Even Nevsky found it difficult to imagine that Leo had been brave in his youth. When the tsar next spoke, he grew angry once more. "Don't you understand, Bishop? Don't any of you care? It seems not even God cares. Enough of all this wasted piety. Why, for just one son, I'd leave half my kingdom to Dhiavol!"

The doors flew open.

A howling wind blew out all the torches, then hurled boyars and warriors against walls and toppled Starik from his perch. He gasped for breath while the wind wrapped burning fingers about his throat. Boyars tried to pull off their golden chains because

the links glowed like embers. Scorched flesh filled the room with the smell of fear. Sovah began to hoot and screech. Battling invisible enemies, he flew overhead. His cries terrified the boyars, who were huddling with warriors. Tserkov fell to his knees and clutched his cross. It was burning through his robe to singe the white hairs on his chest. Icons fell from the walls.

Katrina threw herself at Nevsky. She wrapped her arms about his neck, for only he could stand in the hot wind's path. With his crook dug into the inlaid floor, he intoned: *"Eedee kh chortoo!"* – "Be off with you!" – and he repeated the words in a voice that curdled blood: *"Eedee kh chortoo!"*

The wind died, but only for a moment. Then, blowing with even greater force, it howled like a hundred warlocks casting spells; like a thousand wolves baying at the moon.

In the palace tower, high above, Tsaritsa Elena gathered her daughters about her. Unable to enter, the wind buffeted the tower and its timbers creaked. Even as the mica panes of the windows began to melt, the cathedral bell began to toll.

In the throne room, Tserkov shouted, "No, not my – !" He clutched a pillar and tried to rise but could not.

"I spoke in jest!" Leo cried. The wind snatched away his words. Others shrivelled in his mouth like cinders to scratch his throat when he swallowed. His throne toppled.

In the tower, Katrina's six younger sisters ran screaming from their room. Elena stood rooted to the floor. When the last pane melted, the wind swirled about her, then swept her bobbin into a candle. Yard after yard of lace caught fire before her eyes. A month's painstaking work burned for every toll of the bell. At the thirteenth and last toll, she swooned.

The falcon above Leo's throne also fell, and the two heads broke apart. They rolled to Nevsky's feet even as the wind died.

Coughing and sputtering, Tserkov rose at last. Warriors helped boyars rise while Preestav coaxed Starik out from under the bearskin rug. Both of them bawled for the torches to be lit, yet no one moved. Every courtier was babbling his own version of what had taken place.

Pavel ran into the throne room with his sword unsheathed and half a dozen guards in tow. Grasping Katrina's arm, he asked, "Are you hurt?"

She was about to shake her head, then broke away. "The queen!" she cried.

He followed her into the corridor and headed for the tower stairs.

Nevsky picked up the falcon heads and examined

them. The gold had melted and left jagged edges so that the heads no longer fit back to back. He tossed them toward the throne.

After everyone stopped babbling and the torches blazed once more, Sovah alighted on Nevsky's shoulder to stare at Leo. "Who?" Sovah asked.

To Leo, it sounded like, "Fool."

He cried, "I meant no harm. I only meant —"

Nevsky pounded his crook on the floor. "Enough," he said. "A hundred words of repentance, a thousand prayers on your bare knees won't erase one word spoken in haste!"

Tserkov bowed in dismay over broken icons, which the guards had piled in a corner. He, too, tried to fit pieces together but he, too, gave up. "Sire," he said loudly, facing Leo once more, "you turned your back on God."

"Worse," Nevsky added, "you turned your back on Mir. If I can guess how Dhiavol plots —" Everyone made the sign of the cross, but the hot wind did not blow, for only he could say this dreaded name without fear. " — you'll have your son. I hope he makes you happy." Nevsky turned and left the throne room with Tserkov clutching his shoulder.

They heard Leo call, "I meant nothing by it! Starik, don't forget to write that down!"

Nevsky turned in the corridor. "The scribe won't forget, sire. Nor will your people forget this day for a long, long time. But they'll wish to God they could." At this he raised his crook, and the doors slammed shut.

CHAPTER 4:
NEVSKY'S REWARD

FOR ALL OF NEVSKY'S CLEVER WORDS, HE SAT sleepless that night near the fireplace in the bishop's main room and puzzled over Leo's thoughtless words. Would Dhiavol truly send the tsar a boy? If so, what would he be: an unholy fool, or a prince with such a faint heart that he would gladly surrender half the kingdom? Nevsky searched for answers in the fire but saw nothing in the leaping flames. He fell asleep even as the first birds of morning called animals and men awake.

Sovah returned from his dawn flight to announce, "All the ravens in Mir are on the wing. We should return home."

"We should also stay here," Nevsky said, "in case Leo needs our protection from them."

Sovah hopped onto Nevsky's shoulder and

plucked at the necklace of bear's teeth. "The ravens aren't flying here," he said. "They're heading for the left bank. For Dherevnia."

After bidding Tserkov farewell, Nevsky left Goroth. With the coming of Easter, ice had melted off the Reekah overnight. The early spring road was even muddier than the road of late winter. Peasants stood on the edges of their fields and wondered when they could begin sowing their crops. Children pointed at the ravens, which flew north. When Nevsky reached the forest, he could no longer hear the songs of birds through all the caw-cawing.

"Ravens with raven hearts!" Sovah declared. "They make a noise fit to wake the dead."

Nevsky shouted, "Let's be quick!" He splashed through puddles and leapt ruts and holes.

By the time he reached Dherevnia, at noon, hundreds of ravens circled over the village. Their black cloud cast a pall on one cabin alone: that of Boolochnik. Villagers were throwing stones at the ravens, which caught the stones and rained them like deadly hail on the villagers. Pointing at the cloud, Nevsky shouted words that barely carried in the din, but Sovah understood.

He spun so quickly that he blurred. When he stopped spinning, he was no longer an owl. He had become a hawk. As quietly as a sprite, he flew above the ravens — so high that the wind rippled his brown feathers and the sun tipped them with gold.

Nevsky elbowed his way through the villagers and entered the cabin.

Boolochnik was stooped over a bed in a corner of the one large room. Wringing his hands, he spoke with Father Sashenik, who searched in vain for comforting words.

"What's the matter here?" Nevsky asked.

"You!" Boolochnik cried. "Haven't I had enough ill luck for one day without you coming in here? I knew this would happen. Only yesterday, a hare crossed my path while I was gathering wood."

Marya's black hair lay strewn across her pillow while she moaned and wept, while she tossed in her sleep. Beside her lay a small bundle.

When Nevsky said, "I can help her," Father Sashenik tried to stop him, but he slipped through the priest's arms. Nevsky placed a hand on Marya's brow, which was slick with sweat like the coat of a mare ridden to exhaustion. "Dream no more," he whispered.

She sighed and lay still.

Boolochnik stared at Nevsky as if with new eyes. "I don't know if you're a physician or a magician," the baker said, "but thank you." He looked at the small bundle. "Marya gave birth at dawn to a girl.

That's when those evil birds began to frighten her."
He covered his ears and cried, "That noise, make it
stop!"

"Sovah will deal with the ravens," Nevsky said.

No sooner had he spoken than a screech silenced
the din. Father Sashenik made the two-fingered sign
of the cross, but Nevsky laughed. "There's no need,"
he said. "Watch." He opened a shutter, and they
peered up through the mica panes.

With another screech, Sovah smashed through
the ravens. Black feathers filled the air, and the villagers cheered. Then they fell silent, for the cloud
had torn in half. The ravens were attacking Sovah
from two sides now. He spun once more. Faster and
faster he spun till a windstorm sucked the ravens
into its midst. The wind sucked leaves and twigs,
pine needles and bark into a towering black funnel.
When Sovah stopped spinning, the people cheered
again. He rose with a raven impaled on each of his
talons. Even as he pecked the black birds off, one by
one, the cloud tore into pieces, and the ravens fled.

"How dare you?" Sovah called after them. "Who
invited you?"

The villagers woke Marya with their cheers. They
crowded into the cabin to heap their praises on
Boolochnik. After he described what had happened,
Marya also thanked Nevsky. "Petya," she ordered,

"give him a sweet loaf as his reward."

"Yes, bring the sweet bread and honey!" the butcher declared. "I'll pay for all of it." He wiped his hands on the bloodstained apron flapping in front of his stomach. The more people laughed with him, the more he patted his stomach and beamed with his newfound generosity.

Not to be outdone by the butcher, the milkmaid told her husband, "Bring kvass and mead. Let's celebrate!"

Someone played a pipe; another waved a tambourine. Villagers crowded about the bed to look at the new baby, and when Marya finally revealed the small pink face, they cooed like doves.

When Nevsky tried to look as well, the butcher forgot his good humour. "Go!" he snarled, pushing Nevsky away. "We don't need your sorcery now. Make him leave, Petya Ivanovich! He'll spoil your loaves so they won't rise."

"It's the truth," the milkmaid said. "He spoke to my cows once, when he passed them on the road to Goroth. The very next morning, the milk they gave turned sour."

"Because you let them graze in the weeds," Nevsky said. "I merely told your cows – Oh, never mind." He turned to leave.

Fearful of losing his neighbours' goodwill by

obeying Marya, Boolochnik turned on Nevsky and caught him by the collar. "Did I say you could enter my house?" he asked. "No evil eye may look on my daughter before she's been christened!"

Nevsky pulled loose and once more tried to leave, but villagers blocked his path.

"That's the way," the milkmaid said. "The only way to speak to the likes of him!" She spat on the muddy wooden floor.

"Good riddance," the butcher said. "He likely came to help Dhiavol steal the baby's soul."

At this, Nevsky cried, "Take back those words!"

The oven doors flew open. With a sudden, startling poof, the fire that warmed the cabin began to blaze. But instead of drifting up and out the chimney, smoke filled the room. Everyone coughed and tried to rush outside, while those outside pressed forward to see what went on inside. Boolochnik tried to shut the oven doors and burned his hands. Gasping with pain, he stumbled back. Father Sashenik fell to his knees and feebly made sign after sign of the cross. Nevsky alone dashed for the bed. When the smoke cleared, the butcher and the milkmaid opened their mouths to curse him, but fear made them mute. In the middle of the cabin stood Dhiavol himself.

He had a boar's head, and from his chin hung a

black goat's beard. Slime dripped from his leathery lips. The horns of a ram grazed scaly dragon wings that were sprouting from his back, and a long tail coiled about his neck. The tail was a hissing, darting snake. He had a manlike body covered with barbed spines, and the haunches of a goat. While his wings grew to their full length, his hooves scorched the floor.

Everyone closed their eyes and hoped that this would chase him off. Nevsky alone kept his eyes open.

When Dhiavol shrieked, "Give me the child!" his breath swirled like a hot, howling wind. He, too, made for the bed.

Standing his ground, Nevsky cried, "Never!"

Dhiavol stopped in his tracks. "Ah, Goatherd," he said, "we meet again. I should have claimed you to herd my flock the first time we met."

"Why didn't you?" Nevsky asked.

Dhiavol pointed at the baby, whom Marya had left for the safety of Boolochnik's arms. "I want her soul," Dhiavol said.

"T-take it," Boolochnik offered. He crouched with Marya behind Father Sashenik. Even the priest kept his eyes shut.

"Yes," the butcher cried. "Take the baby and the mad boy!" He was cowering with the milkmaid near the door.

"You fools," Nevsky scoffed. "This child's soul is worth all of yours cast in gold! Why else would Dhiavol himself try to claim it? Yes, take my soul," he offered. "If you can."

Dhiavol took another step forward. Hot breath wheezed from nostrils that flared like those of a wolf. He stank like a hundred corpses rotting in the sun. His yellow eyes blazed as if they could burn Nevsky's in their sockets; as if they could char the flesh from his bones.

Nevsky laughed, then gripped his crook with both hands to form a barrier. Screaming with fury, Dhiavol lunged. He smashed a pawlike hand on the crook, but it would not budge. He kicked, but Nevsky parried. Nevsky caught a hoof in the curve of the crook and pulled Dhiavol off balance. The Evil One fell with a crash through the floor. While he climbed out of the pit and wiped termites from his hide, Nevsky examined the end of his crook, which looked like a staff now. The curved end had broken off, and the jagged wood had charred. "Why do you want her?" he asked.

Dhiavol eyed Nevsky with his head down; with his horns curving into the air. "Because," he said, and he charged.

Nevsky held the crook, no longer a crook but a staff, with both hands. Even as it lifted him to the beams, Dhiavol smashed into a wall. The cabin shook. First an axe, then an icon – both of them fell. Dhiavol whirled and his tail lashed out. It wrapped itself onto the staff to pull Nevsky down. The snake opened its mouth to reveal poisonous fangs.

Nevsky dug in his heels. He dug them into the hoofprints on the floor. "Why won't it bite?" he asked, eyeing the snake. He pulled the staff free and waved the charred end at Dhiavol. "We both know why, Evil One. Listen to me: *Udhar menya nojhom ee platch! Rahnee menya ee umreeh!* Listen to me!" Now he chanted, and everyone understood his words though not their meaning:

> *Stab me and cry,*
> *Wound me and die,*
> *For only one of us is true,*
> *While the other is a lie!*

Dhiavol shrieked. He covered his batlike ears with his pawlike hands, and he howled, "Where did you learn that?"

Nevsky grinned like one who was possessed. Forcing his enemy toward the pit, he said, "In Uroth Peshchera, where I learned my first lessons and began my long task of learning the rest. Back, Dhiavol. Only I can call you that and not endanger my soul. I'm not like the rest, who fear you, yet say your name in vain. Back!"

Dhiavol teetered on the edge of the pit.

Nevsky swung his staff like a heavy, two-handed sword. When he gashed Dhiavol's breast, flames dripped from the wound. Howling with fury, Dhiavol fell backward and down.

Nevsky also fell back, against the bed, and clutched his own breast. Blood began staining his shirt. The staff rolled from his numbed fingers. "Sovah," he cried. "Now!"

As he had through the ravens, Sovah dove at the cabin and smashed through the unshuttered window. Splinters of mica caught in Father Sashenik's beard. Mist trailed from the tips of Sovah's wings to form a snow-white cloud. The snake that was Dhiavol's tail lunged for Sovah, and he pecked out its eyes.

Nevsky pointed feebly at the cloud. It silently burst.

The pure rain hissed when it struck Dhiavol, and he writhed in agony. He climbed from the pit, staggered, and fell to his goatlike knees. "Keep the girl," he moaned. Then he scooped up the snake's eyes and swallowed them whole. "I'll get her one day! The day this kingdom descends to mine in flames."

Smoke surrounded him till only the darting tail showed, the snake's head dripping blood. The smoke rushed up the chimney with a whoosh, and Dhiavol was gone.

After it stopped raining, everyone spoke at once.

Villagers outside called, "What happened in there?" Villagers inside yelled, "Didn't you see?"

Nevsky sighed. He needed to gather his strength for the long climb past the falls, back to his home. There he could fall into his bed of pine boughs and moss. There, he could sleep.

But the people were not done with him.

"I told you," the butcher said. "Evil follows in his wake."

"What did you see with your eyes shut?" Nevsky scoffed.

"Drive him out!" the milkmaid screamed. She snatched up a pewter dish and threw it at him. The rim gashed his brow.

More bewildered than pained, he struggled to his feet. When the butcher cuffed him, Nevsky slipped on the wet floor. He crawled outside and tumbled into the muddy road.

All around him, the villagers snarled like wolves eager for blood. Father Sashenik tried to stop them, and so did Marya, but the villagers' shouts drowned out the two feeble voices.

"Stone him!" the milkmaid yelled. When Nevsky tried to rise, she picked up a stone, then flung it so hard that it shattered against his back.

Other villagers flung the stones they had thrown at the ravens. Sovah made to dive at the people, but

Nevsky called him off. Refusing to use his staff for protection, he pulled himself to his feet. Then he stumbled from Dherevnia.

The villagers chased him through the forest to the foot of Byelleeye Falls. Above them, the rainbow quivered with anger. The lowering sun filled the valley with shadows and the villagers with dread. With their curses ringing in his ears, Nevsky climbed Uroth Gorah. Climbed? He staggered, up toward sunlight. Each step jarred his bones; each breath seared his throat. He barely saw where he went – only that he followed a slippery path up out of shadows. Tears filled his eyes. His brow was bloody, and his breast was on fire. He tripped over roots and the fallen trunks of trees. And each time the villagers heard him cry out, they laughed. Only when they lost sight of him in the spray from the falls did they turn back.

But he had not finished with them, oh no. The sun flooded his meadow with soft golden light. Standing at the top of the falls, he shook his fist. He shouted above the water's roar:

"You – fools! You hate me for saying things you can't. Yet you close your eyes when I keep mine open. Burn in hell for all I care!" He wiped the blood and tears from his face onto the muddy sleeve of his coat. He cried, "That's the last time I try to help anyone!" And he turned his back on Mir.

FIRST INTERLUDE:

THE
KEEPER
SCOFFS

OUR COURT — WHICH HAD REMAINED SILENT thus far — erupted in a flurry of voices, of chairs pushed back from tables, and of pounding cups. Only moments before, we had been like children who delight in every twist and turn — spellbound children, who resist the temptation to ask questions of the teller or to speculate on what might happen next. I do not mean to say that children should not do this. As I often remind my daughter when my grandchildren annoy her with their own speculations about the future — a future that, for her, must surely include my abdication — an audience that does not speculate on the different paths a story might take is, at best, half an audience. For it is the beauty of a living, breathing tale that, although its ending may be preordained, it is capable of taking any number of paths toward that end.

Whether the minstrel's tale was such a one – a living, breathing tale that not only entertained and enlightened but also enchanted – I could not yet say. I must confess that during the first part of his tale, my mind was often on other things. Or, rather, on one other thing – a midnight tryst with my betrothed in the garden behind the palace. But once again I digress. I was telling you of our court's response to Nevsky's oath, one made in the aftermath – no, in the full feeling – of pain.

Some lords shouted, "Good for him!" Others claimed, "He'll change his mind soon enough!" Still others groaned over having been awoken as if from a dream. Even the foreign merchants made themselves heard, in dry voices that called for wine. And the hounds awoke to snuffle near our feet in the hope of further scraps.

Before long, conversation at the head table, where I sat, grew as animated as elsewhere in the hall. One of the ladies near me said, "Imagine, thirteen months' worth of lace gone up in flames!"

To this another lady added, "Imagine being cooped in a tower. It's a wonder that Elena didn't take holy orders!"

Both ladies tittered while they glanced at our throne. I pretended not to have heard, for it was an unwritten rule that no one should allude to the old queen's virginity except in a manner that cast it in a respectful – no, a sacred – light.

As for the queen, she did not budge until the steward admitted himself behind the curtain. Hers was the only cup he would refill without having to be asked – he guarded his keys to the cellar so tenaciously. Then she looked my way and I fancied, through the gossamer that hid her feelings as artfully as it blurred her features, that she was delighted. Though whether by the minstrel's tale or by the passions it had aroused in our court, I could not guess.

From his own, distant table, my beloved eyed me as though urging me to restore order. If not to plead for silence, then to command. It is true that we longed to be married, but there were times I considered finding some other man to groom as prince. Whom, I could not say, but it would have been one who did not know me as well as my betrothed did. Then again, had we not known one another so well, perhaps we would not have been in love, for I must confess that despite our virtue amid the fires of lust, each of us saw in the other what we lacked in ourselves. He was *anima* to my *animus*. We longed to marry so that we could each feel whole, and even if this was the only source of our love, I welcomed it, for throughout my girlhood and youth, I had felt –

and still did feel in my chancellery days – incomplete.

This, too, is something that my daughter does not understand. She thinks that a woman born to be a queen must be sufficient unto herself, with no need of lover or prince, but when I think how lonely the old queen must have been, I am convinced that she would gladly have exchanged her crown for the love of one good man. Even some dullard.

But to return to the unspoken words that my beloved was casting my way, I did nothing to stop the uproar if only because the minstrel seemed unmoved by it. True, he rubbed the left side of his face, but he did not do so with agitation. Rather, I believe it was an innocent gesture, one meant to urge the colour back to his ashen cheek. Indeed, he must have expected the uproar because, as he had told us early on, ours was not the first court in which he had told this tale. And now, even as he licked his dry lips, I commanded the steward to refill the old man's cup.

Some time passed. Many courtiers had risen. They had bowed toward the throne and had left, singly or in pairs, and had returned while straightening their leggings or gowns.

"You see?" a lord told another while we waited for the court to compose itself. "Try to help a peasant!"

To which his fellow asked, loudly so that all could

hear, "What can you expect from people ruled by a foolish king? Making a pact with the devil! Though it seems to me that this kingdom was so idyllic that something had to happen to disturb its tranquility. Otherwise, there would be no tale to speak of."

"By which I suppose you mean," his friend said, "that if the king had not made his pact with the devil – an unwitting pact, mind you – his people would still have brought some curse upon themselves. For as we all know," he added, bowing in the old queen's direction, "a people receive from God the ruler they deserve, and we are surely blessed to be ruled by a monarch as wise and kind as our own. Now, there is a tale worth telling."

Many courtiers congratulated him on displaying such wit, and the camaraderie brought about by the minstrel's tale would have grown had it not been interrupted by a loud, "Bah!"

This exclamation burst from a courtier who had been among the first to leave the hall and was now among the last to return. He said, "Anyone who can read – and there are a few among us with this gift – knows what will happen next."

Despite my inclination to dismiss his words as mere bombast, I did not. He was the Keeper of the Queen's Library and a friend, though I doubt a trusted one, of my betrothed. The keeper strutted back to his place with all eyes upon him, and a lady who could not decipher the mystery he had posed cried, "Tell us!"

He shrugged before saying, "It's clear enough to me. The luckless king will have his prince, an evil prince, and Nevsky will fight him to the death."

"But what about this devil?" my beloved asked. "This Dhiavol. Will he stand by and watch Nevsky defeat the evil son without lifting a hand – or should I say a paw – to help?"

The keeper must not have bargained on being challenged, especially by a friend, for he scowled while inventing a riposte. Then, after snapping his clumsy fingers – fingers that scuffed the gilt on every page he turned in our palace library – he exclaimed, "The bishop! No devil can fight a church. The bishop's clearly an important figure, else why would Nevsky have met him first upon entering Goroth?"

"In fact," my betrothed said, "Nevsky met the toll collector first, though it's true that this was on the bridge and not in the town itself." To show that he was every bit as clever as the keeper, my love added, "Surely everyone present marked the fact that, though Nevsky opened the toll collector's eyes, he was never again as jolly as he once had been? Had I the wit of our blind friend here," my beloved said, nodding in the minstrel's direction, "I should drop more hints that we are in for further disappointment. Or rather, that the many characters in this tale risk further disappointment, however idyllic their lives may be."

Fully aware that he was losing his audience, the keeper looked at one of the banners of pale orange silk on which were embroidered the blue-green eagle of the old queen's reign. By this he showed that he begged leave to address her, and so everyone fell silent. "Your Majesty," he asked, "might we not be more at ease in our beds, dreaming our own dreams, than listening to some tale that has been repeated so often that it holds no surprises for its teller? After all, if it holds no surprises for its teller, it can surely hold few surprises for us, even if this is the first time we have heard it."

He waited, hugging himself for having once more taken the centre of the stage that passed for our court, while the queen, with her head tilted, spoke to her lady-in-waiting. She, in turn, hurried to me, and I bent my head in as regal a fashion as I could muster in order to receive the message. "Her Majesty sends her compliments," the lady-in-waiting said, "and asks that the minstrel be allowed to continue."

There it was, then.

I rose with my chain of office clinking once more and the minstrel, whom I thought had been drowsing through most of these exchanges, fixed his sightless eyes upon me. Even as I intoned, "My lords, ladies, and merchants, I pray you take your seats," his lips twitched in amusement over my latest attempt to speak for our queen.

Muttering, "Oh, very well," the keeper relinquished the floor. However, unlike my betrothed, who looked torn between wanting the tale to continue and keeping our habitual tryst, the keeper leaned back with his arms crossed and his eyes closed.

"Minstrel?" I called. "I trust we have not caused you to drop even a single thread of your tale?"

"Have no fear, Lady Chancellor," he said. "It is not a tale I am likely to forget. Nor, I hope, will you." He finished his wine, smacked his lips, and plucked his harp. Once again he cast a spell from which we could not awaken until the queen should retire to her chambers. Once again he transported us – a few less willingly than the rest, it is true – back to the Kingdom of Mir.

PART TWO:

THE
LONG
MIRROR

CHAPTER 5:
ThE BAKER'S SACRIFICE

NEVSKY LIT A FIRE IN THE MOUTH OF Uroth Peshchera. He crumbled roots while heating water in a pot. Once the water began bubbling, he added the roots to make a potion, then pulled off his coat and bloodstained shirt. A gash snaked across his breast from his right shoulder toward his heart.

"You shouldn't have hit Dhiavol so hard," Sovah said. An owl once more, he blinked his large eyes at the meadow. No one dared climb Uroth Gorah, especially at night, but he still kept watch.

"I forgot my own words in the heat of the battle," Nevsky said. "Any blow we strike against others will hurt us, too. I forgot this, and so I foolishly struck my enemy." He soaked his shirt in the potion, which was as bitter as the taste in his mouth. After he pressed the shirt to his breast, the pain vanished. He sat leaning against the mouth of the cave and bathed his brow and back — one bloody, the other bruised — but the potion had no power against wounds inflicted by mortals. The gash on his breast healed at once and left a scar, one as jagged as a lightning bolt. "I also forgot I have the strength of a man," he said. "By felling Dhiavol, I also felled myself."

"True, but you remembered this too late," Sovah said. "I've read the bishop's thoughts many a time. He believes you have much to learn. I believe this, too."

Nevsky toyed with the key on the necklace of bear's teeth. "Should I pay another visit beyond the door?" he asked.

Sovah said nothing.

Nevsky's thoughts turned to Goroth. Who knew what evil might befall Mir thanks to Leo's unwitting pact with Dhiavol? War, famine and pestilence — these were the scourges of mankind. But more than these, Nevsky feared fire, and fire was Dhiavol's weapon, one so powerful that no red rooster painted above a door could save a house that he had cursed. Still, Nevsky swore that the people of Mir could burn in the fires of hell, so long as Dhiavol left the land itself untouched.

Nevsky lived in a cave now, but if the entire

kingdom were his, he would raze every building except the cathedral. He could destroy the villages and watch the forest grow back. He could watch fields of grain vanish under grass on the steppes. The more he thought about how people spoiled the land – how they packed the soil with their plodding feet till it could not breathe – the more angry he felt. He began to sob, but the more he sobbed, the more his body ached, so he forced the anger from his mind. At last, he fell into a welcome sleep that soon grew fitful. Pain filled his dreams, yet he could no more stop himself from dreaming than he could stop the tears that follow pain.

He dreamt he rode a mare across a steppe. He dreamt he rode between rivers that were too wide to cross. He dreamt he could not turn back. While the mare's hooves churned up rich black soil, a north wind whipped at his cloak and hair and made his eyes water. Yet he felt happy, for in the north loomed a forested hill. It was freshly green and royally purple, and on its peak shimmered a white castle with three towers. Many miles separated him from the castle, but he could see a girl standing at the window of the west tower. She held a lighted candle whose beeswax he could already smell. When the flame flickered across her face, he saw that the girl looked like no one he knew. He urged the mare onward, and she whinnied as if to say, "Yes, home."

Four horsemen appeared at the foot of the forested hill. They rode onto the steppe. They looked like cossacks – warriors who would rove the steppes long after his own time. He knew them from other dreams. One of the cossacks was galloping straight for him. Nevsky tried to turn, but now the rivers boiled. Riding a white horse, the cossack waved an axe, gnashed his teeth, and screamed. When Nevsky pointed his staff at the cossack, a flock of doves flew from the charred end. They flew thickly about the white horse and frightened it into throwing its rider. It rolled over him, and the axe clove the cossack's skull. Yet no blood stained the ground, for the skull of the cossack – this bringer of destruction through conquest – gaped like an empty goblet.

The mare leapt the fallen horse and made for the hill.

The second cossack charged. He was the bringer of famine. He rode a pitch-black horse and waved a flail. His cheeks were sunken, his tongue shrivelled, and his eyes sunk in their sockets. Once again, Nevsky pointed his staff. This time, a field of wheat grew so thickly that it felled the horse and strangled the rider.

The mare leapt once more. The candle flickered in the east tower now, and the girl still smiled.

The third cossack spurred his horse forward. Its coat was a pale yellowish green. He held no weapon, but even as he rode, rats swarmed over him and scraped his face from his skull. They stripped his flesh from his bones, and it hung in shreds from his outstretched hands. This cossack brought pestilence wherever he rode.

For a third time, Nevsky pointed his staff. A lake formed around the pale horse, and its hooves skimmed over ice. A man rose through the surface with frost clinging to his beard. He looked like Tserkov. When he made the sign of the cross, incense rose from the lake. The ice melted, and the horse, the rider, and the rats – all of them drowned. The bishop walked across the lake and out of sight.

Only one cossack remained: the bringer of destruction through war. His red horse sprouted wings and took to the air. Bending low from his saddle, he swung a scythe. Nevsky urged the mare to wheel away, but she took him straight into the scythe's path. The curved blade arced downward and pierced his chest. The point broke off in his heart. When the sun exploded in his eyes, he toppled backward, out of his saddle.

Lying on the steppe, he watched pieces of the sun rise into the darkening dome of the sky. The mare nudged him, but he could not move. He traced patterns in the brightening stars and saw these stars for what they were: faraway suns with worlds that spun while they circled. He would reach one soon, but he wanted to speak to the girl before he died. He wanted to make the journey with her to another, happier world. Then he heard a screeching hoot that sounded familiar. Sovah dove from a white cloud, grasped the blade with his beak, and wrenched it out.

Nevsky leapt back into his saddle.

He rode from the steppe into a forest, where he sheltered his face from branches. At last, the mare stopped at the foot of the hill, and here he looked up. The girl stood in the tallest of the three towers now. When a bat frightened her, she dropped the candle, and fire raged down the hillside. The mare reared and whinnied. Deer and bears, wolves and birds – all fled toward the steppe while the fire destroyed their homes.

Nevsky waved his staff. A single dove appeared and flew to its death in the flames. Wheat sprang up among the trees and caught fire. Water fell from the sky and turned to steam. He called for Sovah, but Sovah did not reply. After calming the mare, Nevsky buried his face in her mane and forced her to climb. Fire crackled in the treetops, smoke hid the castle from sight, but he could hear the girl. He knew she was waiting for him to rescue her. She called a word once, twice. He thought it was his name till he heard it so clearly that she might have been at his side. "Dhurak!" she said, and his heart sank. After all he had done to reach her, even she called him a fool.

He woke with a cry. The fire had nearly gone out, and its embers glowed orange under grey ash. His chest ached when he shivered. Night had settled peacefully on Uroth Gorah, the moon hung over the falls, and yet he felt sad.

"Dhurak," someone shouted, "please come out! Don't make me come any closer."

Sovah fluttered into the cave. "Guess who?" he said.

Nevsky recognized Boolochnik's voice when he repeated, "Dhurak?"

"That's not my proper name," Nevsky called. "What do you want?" He lit a pine torch from a glowing ember and planted the torch in the ground. When light filled the cave, it looked like an ogre breathing fire.

"No," Boolochnik cried. "Don't feed me to the cave!" He fell to his knees beside the Neva. "Have mercy!"

Nevsky laughed without mirth. After he pulled on his goatskin coat and rose, Boolochnik also rose, then slowly approached. They met in the middle of the meadow. Bandages covered the baker's hands, and his fingers could not bend to grasp the bundle pressed to his heart.

"What's this?" Nevsky asked. "A sacrifice to Uroth Peshchera?"

"Don't make fun of me!" Boolochnik cried. He could not tear his eyes from the glowing, grinning cave. He wore a sheepskin coat and felt hat, and yet he shivered. Offering the bundle, he said, "Take the child, please."

Nevsky stared in disbelief. "Now who's mad?" he asked. "What do I want with your daughter?"

"You saved her once, Dhurak. Master Nevsky, I mean. Now save her once again. The villagers say that she'll bring ill luck to Dherevnia. We'll be overrun by hares, they say. Rats will feast on our bones. They wanted me to leave her out to be devoured by wolves, but how can I? They wouldn't even let Father Sashenik christen her, and so her soul will burn in hell."

Nevsky demanded, "What?" Then he scowled and said, "Go back to your ignorant friends and take the child with you. She'll bring far less misfortune than their superstitions will. Raise her to eat and drink and bear you grandchildren with soft heads." Returning along the stream, he walked slowly, for his bruised back ached. He told the forest, "Sovah's the only friend I need."

"Who?" Sovah asked.

To Boolochnik, it sounded like, "Not true."

"Listen," the baker shouted. "I'll keep my best loaves for you – wheat and poppy seed – if you'll come for them at night. I'll give you the most precious things a man can find in the forest: honey and beeswax and furs. I-I'll even give you what little gold I have. Just take her!"

Nevsky looked at the sky and mocked the poor man. "Why, Petya Ivanovich," he said, "do you want the first-born of an illustrious baker to grow up in a cave? To sleep on pine boughs and bathe in a stream? To live with a mad boy and an owl, on roots and nuts and charity?" Laughing with scorn, Nevsky entered the cave and stoked the dying fire to life.

Boolochnik's legs refused to carry him a step closer to Uroth Peshchera. The ivy covering the cave looked like dark green scales, and the fire cast eerie shadows on its deep-set fangs. "All right then," he called. "I'll leave her here. Even if wolves don't devour her, she'll freeze by morning!"

Nevsky crossed his arms and glared at the door in the back of the cave. When he spoke, his voice echoed. "Am I an old woman," he asked, "who nurses every foundling in Mir?"

Sovah watched Boolochnik waiting for Nevsky to

relent. "I shouldn't stay any longer," the baker thought. "Dhurak might feed me to the cave. That's why he wants me to enter." Boolochnik lay the bundle on the grass. Then he turned and ran. He kept his distance even from the Neva so that the cave could not trap him with its tongue.

Sovah hopped onto Nevsky's shoulder. "Where's the learned boy my friend?" he asked.

Nevsky refused to answer. His brow throbbed.

"Now who's deaf as well as blind?" Sovah said. "You're acting no better than the villagers did. At least care for the girl till she's older. Then she can care for herself."

"What do I need with a child crawling under-foot?" Nevsky asked. "Crying and wanting my care? I could never leave her to visit Goroth."

"Take her with you, then. The church raises orphans."

Nevsky kicked at a stone and mumbled, "Oh, very well. Bring her here." He turned from the door to face the meadow.

With a whoop, Sovah flew along the stream. He picked up the bundle and returned to place it in Nevsky's lap. When a corner of the blanket fell away to reveal the child's face, Nevsky's heart skipped a beat. He had never seen such a small child. She looked wrinkled, homely, and helpless. A moon-beam lit her puckered red face. She opened her eyes — her lovely hazel eyes — and began to wail. Fearing that he might drop her, he gently rocked the child. Sovah pushed his face close to hers. When he cooed like a dove, she stopped crying. She put a tiny finger in her mouth and gurgled like the stream. Then she began crying once more.

"She's hungry," Sovah said. "Volcheetsa the wolf has cubs. Perhaps she'll suckle the child."

Nevsky barely heard. He marvelled at the tiny head with its downy wisps of hair. He listened to the baby's cries and forgot his gashed brow and bruised back. No matter how much he tried to resist, as long as he heard her voice, he could feel neither sadness nor anger nor pain.

"We need a name for her," he said.

"Who?"

"Is that all you can say? This child must have a name. And it must be different from all other names, for she's like no other child in Mir." She cooed loudly, as Sovah had done. She gurgled as if she understood Nevsky's words. He laughed and said, "My, she's noisy."

"Who?"

"Oh, stop it. Hm, sound. *Shum?* No, our language won't do. She's different, I tell you. What about Greek? *Ekho*. That's it! Ekho." He bent and dipped a cupped hand in the stream. Muttering a prayer neither a priest nor a bishop could have known, he sprinkled three drops on her brow. When she tried to grasp his hand, he laughed and kissed her. How strange: he had never felt happier. His laughter and her cooing rolled along the stream to Byelleeye Falls.

Sovah flew from the cave. He soared and spiralled and dove. He sent bats flapping for safety in the trees while he called across the meadow, "Who? Who? Ekho!"

CHAPTER 6:

IN THE NEW YEAR

SPRING HAD TRULY ARRIVED FOR NEVSKY. Uroth Gorah became the world to him and Uroth Peshchera his palace. To keep out the rain, he set mica panes in the two holes that looked like the ogre's eyes. He spent his days making furniture and spent his evenings carving it with flowers and birds: first a cradle, then a table and chairs, cupboards to line one wall, benches to line the other. He also made himself a proper bed. When Ekho began to crawl, he built a floor of planks above the stream that flowed from the cave.

The animals of the forest gave her gifts. Volcheetsa, the she-wolf, gave milk. Medvyedeetsa, the she-bear, brought a rug made from the skin of her father, who had died in his sleep. Squirrels brought acorns, and birds brought berries and fruit.

Once a week Nevsky visited Dherevnia after nightfall. On each visit, he asked Boolochnik for something, and true to his word the baker gave freely: first a blanket for the cradle, then clothes for Ekho. Even a wicker doll. Nevsky asked nothing for himself, but he gladly took the bread and salt that Boolochnik claimed was from Marya. Summer passed like a dream. When the poplars turned yellow and geese began to leave, Nevsky hung curtains in the cave's mouth to keep out winter's coming chill. He also asked the baker for a stove.

"You want a brick one I suppose?" he demanded. "And who's to carry it up Uroth Gorah?"

"A clay stove will be fine," Nevsky said. "I'll carry it myself."

And so Boolochnik traded two dozen loaves to the village potter for clay tiles. Nevsky hid the load in the forest near Dherevnia, and later that night Sovah brought the tiles to the cave. By next evening, smoke rose from a chimney in the roof. Uroth Peshchera no longer looked like a cave, it looked like a home, and Nevsky renamed it Uroth Domah. Monster Home. At times it seemed that the golden days of autumn would last forever.

On the first day of winter, it began to snow. Frost had triumphed in its battle with the sun, and the north wind blew thick wet flakes. It howled all night and frightened Ekho till Nevsky rocked her to sleep. When he awoke next morning, the silence troubled him. He drew back the curtains, sucked in his breath, and laughed. After tugging on his boots and coat and fur cap, he ran outside to dance. Snow covered only the northern side of the trees. When he looked uphill, the forest looked green and brown; when he looked downhill, the forest looked blue and white; but whatever its colour, it smelled of pine resin. And of woodsmoke from Uroth Gorah.

Sovah woke Ekho and brought her, wrapped in her blanket, to Nevsky. Then Sovah perched like a feathered crest on the fur cap.

"Look, little one, look!" Nevsky cried. She laughed and waved her tiny hands at waxwings, who sang her their first song of winter.

At last, he ran through the snow to the top of Byelleeye Falls. They had not yet frozen, but icicles had begun forming. Like Medvyedeetsa, who slept in her den, the rainbow had gone into hiding. As far as the eye could see, a white blanket covered Mir, and the Reekah wound under a thin layer of ice. It wound past Dherevnia, through the forest and orchards, and toward Goroth. In his mind's eye, he saw houses looking cozy under white mantles, broken only where chimney smoke rose in wavy grey lines. Looking at the eastern bridge, he knew that the toll collector was already at his post – and warning people that the ice was not yet thick enough to save them from grief.

"You'll have to go to Goroth soon," Sovah said. He bent over, and when Nevsky looked up, he saw an owly face against a clear blue sky.

He hugged Ekho to his breast. "I should go before the bishop sends Oleg for me," he said. "I want no tracks but my own in the snow up here." Then he sighed and asked, "When will Tsaritsa Elena deliver her son?"

"In ten days," Sovah replied. "On the first day of the New Year."

Nevsky turned and looked past Uroth Domah. Beyond the cave, the mountain curved sharply upward, and the forest thinned into purple-grey rock. "Ten days before I have to leave," he said. Then he told Ekho, "Come, little one. It's time to get ready for Christmas, for the Mass of Christ. But first, we eat. Then Sovah will cut some boughs to decorate our home. From high up there." He pointed at the crown of a tall fir.

"Why me?" Sovah asked.

"Because I can't fly," Nevsky said.

SIX DAYS after Ekho's first Christmas, Nevsky left reluctantly for Goroth. Sovah remained behind to look after her.

Byelleeye Falls had frozen, so Nevsky climbed down a long ladder he had leaned against the pillars of ice. He had made it by lopping half of the branches off a tree trunk, and he left it in place because no villager dared to climb past the falls. On his back were strapped snowshoes, which he had made from willow and thong, and his staff. Snow covered the now thick ice on the Reekah. Walking so quickly that he seemed to glide, he snowshoed to Goroth in no time.

To celebrate the coming of the New Year, children wore their sheepskin coats inside out and went from house to house collecting sweets. The children held hands and danced around him, but their parents remained aloof.

Goroth did not look as inviting as it once had. Soot from chimneys covered the snow, and the passing weight of feet had churned it into slush. He wanted to buy a gift for Ekho but all the shops were closed, for people had gathered in the town square to celebrate the birth of their prince. Workmen had built three stages in front of the palace gates. On the largest of these stages, buffoons clowned for women and men, while puppets on the smaller stages made the children laugh.

When Nevsky entered the southeast tower of the cathedral, Oleg cried, "If it isn't the young master!" He took the snowshoes and coat but knew better than to touch the staff. Raising his eyebrows in warning, he said, "The old master's in a black mood."

Tserkov looked pleased to see Nevsky, then waved angrily at a window overlooking the square. "How dare they put on plays in front of my cathedral?" he asked. "Is the ritual of Mass not enough for them?"

"These plays are harmless," Nevsky said.

When Tserkov's eyes fell on the charred end of the staff that had once been a goatherd's crook, he exclaimed, "It's true! You did fight the Evil One, just as Father Sashenik said. These village priests spin tales faster than their wives spin yarn. I thought he would never leave. But I want to hear your version of the tale."

"Soon," Nevsky said.

Waiting for Oleg to serve the midday meal, Nevsky and Tserkov sat at the table. On silver plates, Oleg laid out grilled pork, boiled fish, potatoes, and bread. He poured kvass for Nevsky and mead for Tserkov.

Then, while Oleg and Olga listened from the doorway to the kitchen, Nevsky told Tserkov of the battle with Dhiavol and of Ekho's coming to him.

The bishop nodded and smiled. "I've missed you, my son," he said, "but it seems you haven't missed us. No, it's all right. She must be good for you. You've trimmed your hair, I see, and you keep the dirt brushed from your coat."

After this, the conversation turned grim, and the servants left them alone – the young master with the old. Neither Nevsky nor Tserkov doubted that Elena would give birth to a boy, but they could not decide which half of the kingdom Dhiavol would claim from Leo.

"It must be the left," Tserkov said. "Dherevnia is on the left bank, and that's where the Evil One appeared."

Nevsky said nothing. He was wondering, for the first time in months, why Dhiavol had tried to steal Ekho's soul. "Perhaps," he thought, "because she was the first child born after Leo made his unwitting pact." Nevsky was about to say this aloud when a roar sounded in the square.

After he opened the window, he and Tserkov looked outside. The bishop sneezed and drew back from the cold air, but Nevsky remained to watch. Leo stood on the balcony of his palace. With him stood his foremen – his eldest boyars – and Preestav, the bailiff. People flocked toward the iron gates to listen to the tsar. "We should, too," Nevsky said.

Slow as they were to put on their coats, Nevsky and Tserkov found themselves in plenty of time. The people cheered Leo for so long that he could not speak. He grinned while he waved his treelike arms. At last, soon after Nevsky and Tserkov descended the cathedral steps, the crowd fell silent.

"My people," Leo shouted. "For years I've wanted a son. Not for myself, but for you!"

"Does he think Elena's son is his?" Tserkov muttered.

"I have great news," Leo called. "Spread it to the corners of the kingdom. Rejoice! Elena did not give birth to a boy —"

The crowd groaned. "What?" someone called. "Not another girl? I could do better than that!"

Leo shouted, "Elena gave birth to two boys! Twins!"

How the people cheered. A hundred caps flew into the air while Leo grinned and waved. After he vanished into the palace, musicians beat drums and blew horns. Jugglers let chained bears loose to dance in the crowd, and kvass and mead flowed from bottomless jugs.

"Two princes," Nevsky said. "Which one will become tsar?"

Tserkov shrugged. "The one who was born first, of course. Let's wait till later to pay our respects to Elena."

No sooner had he said this than Preestav appeared from the crowd. Although it was cold, he kept his coat open so that people would bow to the gold keys dangling on his breast. "The tsar invites you to the palace," he said — in a manner that conveyed not an invitation but a royal command.

The crowd parted, and Tserkov blessed all those who fell to their knees. The people had no eyes for Nevsky, and he had none for them.

Once inside the palace, Preestav led Nevsky and Tserkov down many long corridors, and Nevsky took his time admiring the craftsmanship. No two doors were alike. One was carved with pine boughs and cones, a second with toadstools, and a third with juniper. Nor were any two torch brackets alike. One was shaped like a frog, another like a turtle, yet another like a fish. In every corridor, as in every cabin in the forest and every hut on the steppes, there hung an icon and an axe.

Leo stood grinning outside Elena's chamber, which was guarded by two warriors. He stood with his hands on his hips; with his robe thrown back to show off a new gold belt. He opened his arms wide. "What a great day for me," he said. "A great day for Mir! Where have you been hiding, Dhurak? No, you're no fool." He told Preestav, "From now on, my wise young friend will be known as Master Nevsky."

"I'll tell Starik to write that down, sire," Preestav said.

Shouting, "Good!" Leo struck his shoulder. Then he told Nevsky and Tserkov, "Come, see my sons. What a way to start a new year! God is good. God is great. We'll have a week of feasting! I'll open the palace gates, and the poor of Goroth will eat in my hall. Roasted beef and boar, pigeon pies and goose. Rye bread and wheat. Vegetables, fruit, sweets, and nuts. Kvass and mead and wine. My mouth waters to think of it! And the poor of the countryside? I'll have my warriors take the food and drink to them." He grinned at the men guarding Elena's door. "Make them work for once! People will remember this day for years." He slapped Tserkov on the back and ruffled Nevsky's hair. Kicking twice at the chamber door, Leo called, "Open! Admit the Bishop of Mir and Master Nevsky. Open for my friends!"

And so the celebrations went on, far into the night and then, as Leo had promised, for seven days.

He named one boy Ikar Lvovich – Ikar, son of Leo – and the other boy Ivan Lvovich – Ivan, son of Leo. When Tserkov christened them in the cathedral, every boyar attended with his lady. So did the merchants of Goroth and the elder of every village. People spent more time looking at one another than they did watching the ceremony. The boyars wore sable or beaver coats and carried matching, high-crowned hats. They kept their coats unbuttoned to show their ceremonial belts, all of them gifts from Leo. The ladies wore brocaded gowns in such dazzling colours that the paintings and mosaics paled. The ladies also wore headbands that stood as high as a bishop's mitre. Precious stones studded these bands, and when the ladies nodded at one another, candlelight flashed from the stones. The gold icons on the royal doors looked like pewter, and only Nevsky saw the vanity of these mortals, who vied with God for attention in His very own house.

As always, Nevsky watched from the back. The white linen shirt over his white linen trousers was belted with gold. Over all this, he wore a wolfskin cloak. Leo had presented them to mark the princes' birth, and for once Nevsky had tried to act grateful. Now, though, he was annoyed. He had to be careful where he sat so he would not dirty his clothes, and his new boots chafed his heels. But Leo did not notice such things.

Holding his sons, he grinned at his subjects as if to say, "See how lucky I am?" He wore his crown jauntily, as if it was a felt hat, but it was not. Made of the finest leather, the crown was trimmed with sable and embroidered with gold thread, and on its top stood a jewelled cross.

Nevsky looked from the crown to Tsarevna Katrina, who stood apart from her six sisters. She stood in Elena's place, for the queen was still recovering from the birth of her sons and could not leave the palace for forty days. Katrina looked sad even with Pavel beside her. She tried to keep her eyes on the altar, but they kept drifting back to the crown. And when the young boyar whispered comments to her, she nodded or tried to smile, but she rarely whispered back.

Watching her reminded Nevsky of Ekho. Katrina also had hazel eyes, but he had yet to see Ekho sad. All at once, the splendour sickened him. He no longer looked forward to the feasting. Here, there was too much fur and not enough wool. At the feast, there would be too much mead and not enough kvass. He longed to rock Ekho's cradle with his foot while he whittled toys for her; longed to watch Sovah bring his feathery face close to her pink one to make her coo.

Without pausing to wonder whom he might disappoint this time, Nevsky slipped outside. By the time the ceremony ended, he had sold his heavy belt and stiff boots for silver to spend on Ekho. By the time the feasting began, he was snowshoeing home. He knew that Leo would be too caught up in himself to miss him, but Nevsky wished he had at least bade Tserkov farewell.

THREE YEARS TO THE DAY after the christening, Leo held a second ritual, one as old as the crown. During these years, Nevsky visited Goroth only three times, and he never took Ekho to the town.

Each time Sovah reminded him that the church raised orphans, Nevsky thought of a reason to keep her. At first, he said, "She's too young for a journey. Let's wait till she's older. Besides, Oleg and Olga won't want her crawling underfoot." Later, he said, "I'll teach her to speak our language. The monks won't have patience for that." And, still later, "Let's wait till she can read and write. The church will value her more." But Sovah was only testing Nevsky's new-found love. True, Nevsky had once sworn that he would never again help anyone, but now he could no more imagine life without Ekho than he could imagine it without Sovah. She needed him, and as he told Sovah one day, "Happy is the man who is needed, for he has reason to wish for a long life."

"Too true," Sovah said.

Then both of them praised Ekho's latest discovery: that no two snowflakes were alike. How quickly she learned, and how much.

She had begun to speak on her very first birthday,

and Nevsky was teaching her the languages of animals and men. After she began to walk, they spent their days trekking through the forest, where they visited Medvyedeetsa in her den and Volcheetsa in her lair. When Ekho grew tired, he carried her. Soon she was climbing trees to visit newly hatched birds in their nests. She was so fearless that she squeezed herself into hollow logs, where bees let her lick honey from their combs. Often, the bees swarmed across her head and wove themselves into a ticklish velvet crown.

Yet nothing made Nevsky happier than when she began to sing. Her songs reminded him of a time long ago, when he had spent his days watching goats and playing a flutelike pipe. He had lost it because he had not taken it with him into the cave, but how could he be sad about something he had lost all those years ago? Birds twittered while Ekho sang, squirrels beat their tails to keep time, and Medvyedeetsa danced. Dherevnia seemed kingdoms and seas away, and Goroth on the edge of the world.

THE SECOND RITUAL began in the throne room. This time only men, Nevsky among them, were allowed to watch. After Preestav led Ikar Lvovich and Ivan

Lvovich into the room, Leo picked them up and put each boy on an arm of the throne. Then the court barber shaved the boys' heads. He left a lock of red hair dangling over one ear as a sign of royal birth. After plaiting the locks, he rubbed each boy's head with oil and Leo told Starik to write, "Neither prince cried."

Although they looked alike, people could easily tell them apart. Elena always dressed Ikar in grey and Ivan in brown. Even she could not say which boy had been born first – which might inherit the crown – and no one seemed to care. As for the physician who had attended their birth, soon after the princes' christening, he had succumbed to the smoke from a fire.

Leo led his sons into the courtyard while the rest of the men followed. Stamping their feet in the snow, two grooms waited. Each held the reins of a pony that smelled of warm stables. The ponies were richly bridled but neither had been saddled. The sky was grey, almost black, and Nevsky hoped for snow while he scratched his chin. He was thirteen now, and his whiskers had begun to grow. They were as soft as down and so black that they looked dark blue.

Watching him, Tserkov shook his head in wonder. Three years had passed, and though he had not seen Sovah in all this time, Tserkov knew that Nevsky and the owl were growing more alike. Not that Nevsky's nose was hooked, but both had all-seeing eyes.

"Up you go!" Leo said. "And you, too!" He placed Ikar on the grey pony and Ivan on the brown. Then Leo addressed the boys for all the court to hear: "One day, you'll ride across the steppes and through the forest, ford streams, and climb the Mountains of Mir. Ride hard, my sons! And now, let us see what we shall see."

Two of his foremen moved in front of the ponies. Each foreman held a cushion on which rested a small sword. They held these cushions so that the princes would have to reach around their ponies' necks for the hilts. Nevsky knew of the ritual. If a prince fell from his mount, he would be given a quill pen and taught to read and write. If he did not fall, he would be taught how to fight and even be allowed to sleep beside his sword.

"I hope they both fall," Nevsky thought. "What does Mir need with more warriors?"

At a signal from Preestav, the princes leaned forward. Like a single prince reflected in a mirror, they pressed their faces into their ponies' manes, leaned sideways to lengthen their reach, and groped for the hilts. Nevsky held his breath. He wanted to shout, "Fall, both of you, now!" But before he could blink, the princes grasped the hilts, sat upright, and waved their swords in the air.

"This is good," Leo cried. "They'll both learn to be warriors!"

After the cheering stopped, Tserkov said, "The prince who does not know how to read or write cannot learn to rule."

"Bah!" Leo said. "I was a warrior in my youth. Only in my old age did I learn to read. And I've never learned to write. There's plenty of time for such things. A man can learn more in a saddle than he can in a chair." He laughed. "That's good! Starik, write that down."

The scribe, who stood bent over his parchment, nodded and wrote.

"Also write," Tserkov said, "that what is written with a pen cannot be hacked away with a sword."

"That's it!" Nevsky cried. The courtiers stared at him as if he had gone mad. "That's the difference between the princes! Don't you see?"

One by one, the courtiers saw what he had finally seen, and they slapped their foreheads for their blindness. The princes sat on their ponies like perfect reflections in a mirror. Ikar held his sword with his right hand while Ivan held his sword with his left. Not even Nevsky could say which of them was real and which of them was merely a reflection of his twin.

Tserkov muttered, "Dear God," while he made the sign of the cross.

CHAPTER 7

SEEDS OF FEAR, FLOWERS OF hATE

THE SUN TRIUMPHED IN ITS BATTLE WITH frost, and ice melted on the river. Medvyedeetsa emerged from her den to dance on Ekho's birthday. Peasants planted and hoed and prayed. The harvest moon rose and set. The forest turned poplar yellow and maple red, and the oaks stood tall and bare. Frost won its battle with the sun, Byelleeye Falls froze, and the rainbow ceased its dance. Then the sun triumphed, once again, in its battle with frost. Year followed year as surely as death must follow life, and over the years a change came over the kingdom. Everyone noticed this, but only Nevsky and Tserkov seemed to care.

Starik called Leo the greatest tsar Mir had known, for Elena had given each side of the Reekah its own prince. Ikar Lvovich came to be called Napravo, or on the right, for when he faced downstream his sword hand protected the right bank. Ivan Lvovich came to be called Levsha, or left-hander. But only when boyars began taking sides did Nevsky and Tserkov begin looking grim. Boyars with estates on the right bank praised Ikar; those with estates on the left praised Ivan. Far removed from Goroth, the peasants cared little about who would be crowned after Leo died, but in Goroth warriors had to stop quarrels from breaking out. No one was killed, so Leo thought these quarrels were harmless. The throne room resounded with laughter, for he was now the jolliest buffoon in Mir.

Each time Nevsky arrived for the princes' birthday, he received yet another gift from Leo. And each time Nevsky tried to warn the tsar, he treated the warnings like jests.

This was still the only time of year that Nevsky would leave Ekho's side. On the morning of their fourteenth New Year's Day together, they broke their fast in silence. She was always sad to see him leave, but today she seemed sadder than ever. She handed him a leather pouch of food, and he kissed her brow. He no longer had to bend to do this, for she stood almost as tall as he.

"Smile for me," he said. "I'll be back tomorrow by noon, as always."

"It's not only your leaving, Master," she said. "It's

just that — I can almost see the cathedral when you paint it with words, but I'd still like to enter it beside you. I'd like to visit Goroth."

He put on his fur cap. Then he waited for her to bundle herself in a cloak before he pulled back the curtains. Sunlight flooded the cave. "There's nothing to see in the town except envy and hatred," he said. "Once, Goroth was a capital place. Now, blacksmiths spend so much time forging weapons that they no longer forge tools. Few people attend Mass because they're all so busy making plans. No one sings in Mir except the peasants and the monks. And you."

He picked up his staff. He barely noticed that it had grown lighter over the years, and that instead of reaching to his head, the top of the staff reached only to his shoulder. He was twenty-three now and had reached his full height — although, having been born a peasant, he was shorter and stockier than the men of Goroth. "Who's to blame the people?" he said. "They're ruled by a tsar who's blind as well as deaf." Sighing at the weak sun of early winter, he struck the ground with the staff. "No, they're also to blame. They've forgotten their true enemy. If only I could fight him, but he has so many warriors, and I have none."

Ekho smiled at last and threw her arms about his neck. "You have me and Sovah!" she said. She toyed

with the collar of his wolfskin cloak.

"Who?" Sovah asked. He was perched on the back of her chair. To both of them, it sounded like, "True."

Nevsky gazed into her hazel eyes. Her face was no longer round; it was shaped like an acorn. And her chestnut hair had grown so long that she could sit on the silky ends.

She said once more, "You have me and Sovah."

Shaking his head, he asked, "What good will that do our people?"

She closed the front of his cloak and patted his chest. Even through the fur and the linen shirt, she could feel the necklace of bear's teeth and the iron key. As she had many times over the years, she asked, "What's beyond the door?"

And as he had each time, he answered, "A passage." This had become a game with them, but for once he could not smile.

"And at the end of the passage?" she asked.

"Another cave."

"And outside that cave?"

"A place only Sovah and I have seen."

Now she should have said, "What's it like?" But she surprised him by asking, "Is it evil?" He looked silently past her at the cave's fangs. When he tried to leave, she held him and spoke: "Ever since the ritual of the swords, you've gone beyond the door each night you've returned from Goroth. But Sovah stays here, and he won't answer when I ask him why." Looking at the door, she shivered. "And each time you return to us, your beard has grown – as if you've spent weeks there. How long that single night feels to me. Then you mutter in your sleep and later write out spells. Why do you go, Master, if it's evil?"

While she spoke, he looked at her with new eyes, for she had seen more than he had hoped she would see. This was why, instead of trying to shelter her with answers that told her little, he told her the truth:

"Because only by looking evil in the face can I tell it apart from good. Too often, they appear the same." He turned from her and waved beyond the snow-white meadow. "The boyars are ready to fight. I can feel it. That's good if they're preparing to defend Mir from enemies, and yet the mountains defend us better than any weapon can. Each side of the river wants what belongs to the other. That's not good. Worse, it's evil." Turning back to her, he said, "There's a time to fight and a time to lay down arms –"

Now she turned away. "Often I understand you, Master, but sometimes I don't." Brightening, she faced him again. "Why don't you give me the key?

By the time you return from Goroth, I'll be nearly as wise as you."

"No! Never!" He tried to kiss her forehead, but she refused to look at him even when he stroked her silky hair, bunched above the collar of her cloak. At last he lifted her chin, so her eyes could meet his. "I don't want you to become like me," he said. "You would grow older than your years, as I did. Sometimes I wish I'd never —" He looked past her at Sovah, who was staring at him.

Sovah said in a language that Ekho did not speak, "Don't be a fool. If you'd never entered this cave, you could not have saved her soul."

"Wish you'd never what?" she asked.

"Told you," Nevsky said, "about the passage to that other world. Try to forget it. I'll bring back a curtain we can hang in front of the door. We'll pretend it's no longer there." He picked up his snowshoes. "Now, what else shall I bring you from Goroth?"

"Only yourself," she said, cheery once more. "But quickly."

And so he ran across the meadow to the top of the falls. Here he clambered down the ladder he had made. The ice green pillars of the frozen falls reminded him of the hazel of her eyes. "She really is like the land," he thought. "No, not like the land. It rarely changes from year to year while she grows more lovely." Memories of all their happy times sped him on his snowshoes down the Reekah.

When he reached Goroth, he hurried through the town. As the children did each year on this day, they wore their sheepskin coats inside out while collecting sweets, but this year he noticed changes that troubled him. Every man wore a grey or brown feather in his cap. Three crowds, not one, watched the plays in the square. Men wearing the grey feather refused to mingle with men wearing the brown, while the women and children, in the middle of the square, kept their distance from the men.

Later, while Nevsky ate, Tserkov stood at the window. He frowned at the plays, which Nevsky no longer claimed were harmless. "The disease is spreading," Tserkov said. He fingered the cross dangling in front of his long beard. "As a young man I walked only in sunshine, which lingered when I grew old. Now shadows dog my steps and chill my bones. Even the boyars have begun taking sides. Don't they see that warriors aching for battle could destroy this land? Our land. God willing, the boyars will keep their quarrels to the island, not take them into the countryside."

Nevsky swallowed a mouthful of cold roast fowl and sipped at his kvass. "Mmm," he said, but he did not feel content. "The island has bridges," he warned, "and village priests are in town for the celebrations. If the priests carry home the seeds of fear they'll find in Goroth, Dhiavol will harvest flowers of hate."

Tserkov crossed himself, then laughed. "After all this time," he said, "I still forget you're the only one in Mir who can call the Evil One by name." Growing serious once more, he added, "I fear that someday you will say that name once too often, and neither your staff nor your necklace will save you."

Nevsky shrugged while fingering the bear's teeth and then the key. "If only such things could save Mir," he said.

That afternoon, he climbed the palace tower with Leo. "I like being alone with you," the tsar declared. "Everyone else frowns too much, even the bishop." Leo had barely changed since Nevsky had first seen him, in the throne room all those many years ago. True, his moustache, eyebrows, and royal lock had turned to white from reddish grey, yet time could not bend his treelike back.

They passed the room in which Tsaritsa Elena and her daughters spun their lace. Each year, Katrina gave Nevsky the lace she had made so that he could give it to Ekho, and each year he traded it for something more useful: an embroidered apron, a pewter dish. While Leo waited on a landing, Nevsky fingered a torch bracket in the form of a swan. He admired such objects more than ever, for no one made them now. These days, goldsmiths earned their keep by ornamenting helmets, breastplates, and swords.

He and Leo climbed again, then stepped into cooling air. North of the island, the Reekah parted to surround Goroth with ice. On a distant snow-covered hill, three bare oaks rose like gallows awaiting their victims. Not one tree grew in Goroth, for buildings covered the island. From up here, the town was nothing more than rooftops covered with sooty snow and streets filled with slush. "We could never live in this town," he thought. To climb a tree in summer, children had to pay a toll and cross one of the two bridges. He shook his head over the strangeness of some people's lives. Then he turned to look south, past the point of the teardrop on which the palace stood.

Here the Reekah rejoined itself and the steppes began. Four horsemen were galloping north. They were too far away for Nevsky to make out, but the horses looked familiar. The first was white, the second was black, the third was a pale yellowish green, and the fourth was red. He tried to remember where he had seen such horses before but could not.

At times like this, he felt that he had forgotten more than he had ever learned. Worse, he wondered whether anything he had learned could save the people of Mir.

Unlike Nevsky, Leo could not bear silence. He spread his arms to take in both banks of the Reekah. "Was I not right?" he crowed. "My people are happier than ever! Long ago, the bell rang thirteen times to usher in all these years of joy. With more to come, and soon."

"Why joy?" Nevsky asked. "And how many more?"

"Because tonight each side of the river will have its own prince. My sons are young men now. They can call themselves the sons of the tsar, Ikar Tsarevich and Ivan Tsarevich. How my people love them!" Showing teeth yellowed by age, he laughed.

"Sire," Nevsky said, "giving the princes fine new titles changes nothing. They'll remain Napravo and Levsha: on the right, and left-hander. If people in the countryside are happy – and they still are as happy as peasants can be, with such hard lives – it has nothing to do with the princes. The people of Goroth, though, are not at all happy. Why do boyars sharpen their swords?"

"To keep them from growing dull!" Leo's laughter scared off a pigeon that was heading for the tower.

Nevsky stroked his beard. "Why not let their swords go dull?" he said. "We have no fear of attack from other kingdoms. Nothing can cross the mountains except clouds, and no one can sail up or down the gorge. Sire, the boyars are preparing for war. It's the only way to decide who will inherit your crown."

Leo snarled, "You lie!"

Waving his staff over Mir, Nevsky said, "See for yourself. Tomorrow, the boyars will return to their estates to collect their taxes of cattle and furs. And like the village priests, the boyars will sow the seeds of fear. Tradesmen grow rich selling axes and spears and shields. Soon every fur and head of cattle in Mir will belong to the merchants of Goroth. Can't you see? The boyars from the right bank hate Ivan. They call him backward because he's left-handed. The Reekah has become a long mirror, and boyars on either side are growing to hate their reflections. Even if you name one prince as your sole heir, only half the kingdom will –"

"Stop it," Leo roared. "You're ruining my good mood. Everyone tries to ruin my mood! I've barely heard anyone laugh at court since the princes were born. You're the worst. You make my courtiers chuckle with your sayings. 'If this is a church, where is the altar?' Starik reminded me of that only yesterday. But I've rarely seen you smile – you're so busy being clever – and now you've ruined my good mood." He waved a fist in Nevsky's face. "Leave my palace. Guards!"

"You're the one who should leave," Nevsky said. "Just for once, I wish you'd leave your precious island. Not to ride or hunt but to listen to your people. Listen to the women and the children. How they'll wail when their husbands and fathers die!"

On his way down, he heard pounding feet, then passed two warriors. "Hurry!" he snapped, pointing up the stairs. "A pigeon is threatening the tsar."

Furious at Leo, Nevsky returned to the cathedral for his snowshoes and left at once for home. Just as he had sworn, many years ago, never to help anyone again, now he swore that he would never return to Goroth. And yet, like other vows he had made in anger, he would soon break this one. He saw this already and so did Sovah – both of them with their all-seeing eyes.

CHAPTER 8:
LEO THE LUCKY

THE VERY NEXT DAY, AT NOON, NEVSKY SAW A familiar figure at the top of the falls. It was Oleg. "Master Nevsky!" he called. While he ran along the Neva and up the meadow, his heavy boots left wide tracks in the snow. He stopped at the entrance to Uroth Domah and twirled his cap in his hands. Ekho was serving the midday meal, yet he barely saw her. Gasping from his run, he told Nevsky, "You must return – at once. The tsar is dying."

Nevsky showed no surprise. Nor did he want to leave. Ekho had been glad of his early return on the previous evening. During the night, hoarfrost had descended on the forest to turn it into a glassy wonderland. They had walked all morning while Sovah had circled high above them like a hawk. Ekho had skipped beside Nevsky like a child, and their laughter had shaken the hoarfrost off the trees to fill their tracks. Now he followed Oleg's deep tracks to the top of the falls. So did Ekho, sad once more, and Sovah. They watched Nevsky and Oleg backing slowly down the pine-tree ladder.

Oleg had left his sleigh near the foot of the falls. Even as Nevsky approached, the mare whinnied. She stamped so hard that the cloth wrapped around her fetlocks came loose.

He looked up in time to see Sovah swooping past the green-white pillars of ice. "I'm coming, too," he called.

"Stay with Ekho," Nevsky said.

"You'll need me in Goroth."

When the mare whinnied again, Nevsky heard her say, "The girl will be fine."

"Oh, very well," he said.

Turning the mare so she faced downstream, Oleg shook his head. He was used to Nevsky's talking to Sovah as if he was human, but to a mare he barely knew? By the time Oleg had finished retying the cloth about her fetlocks, Sovah was halfway to Goroth.

The sleigh flew down the frozen Reekah. Oleg sat with his face muffled against the wind while Nevsky sat huddled behind him in a bearskin rug. The runners hummed across the snow-covered ice, and the bells jingled, yet he disliked the ride. When he snow-shoed down the river, he had time to see everything. Now it whizzed past in one long blur. Each bend in the river looked like the last, and each peasant fishing on the ice might just as well have been the same peasant. Looking forward to returning home on foot, Nevsky tried not to worry about having left Ekho by herself. What harm could befall her on Uroth Gorah?

Pavel met him in the palace courtyard and helped him out of the sleigh. Nevsky's beard had frozen stiff and felt like the bristles of a brush. Preestav, who waited in the guard room, handed him a goblet of hot mead to thaw his blood. Even as Nevsky combed the ice from his beard with his fingers, he fancied that the stuffed heads on the walls cried, "Hurry!"

"What happened?" he said at last.

Pavel took Nevsky's cloak and handed it to a guard.

Sovah took his place on Nevsky's shoulder.

"No one knows except Starik," Pavel replied, "and he keeps muttering about the old ways. Leo refused to get out of bed this morning. I fetched the court physician." Pavel pushed flaxen hair back from his brow. "I fear our king is tired of life, but why?"

Nevsky hurried through the corridors with Pavel

at his side and Preestav leading the way. The young boyar kept his hand on the hilt of his sword. Walls carved with scenes of country life flashed by as quickly as real life had. At every corner, boyars and warriors whispered among themselves. They fell silent and bowed to Nevsky, but none of them smiled. They looked like wolves planning a kill.

At Leo's chamber, Preestav knocked, and Starik flung open the door.

When the scribe glared at Nevsky's throat, Nevsky shuddered. Starik had often resembled a vulture, and now he sounded like one, as well. "It's all your fault," he screeched. "If it hadn't been for your poisoned counsel, Leo would never have left Goroth. I warned him not to go!"

"Write what you want later," Nevsky said, pushing past Starik. "Let me through."

Sovah hooted at the scribe and flew up to perch on a beam.

Pavel and Preestav remained in the corridor.

A hundred candles burned in Leo's chamber. Light flickered off gold icon covers and bed curtains, yet Nevsky had never seen a gloomier place. Smoke from incense burners hung in clouds, and the floor was slippery with tears.

Leo lay on a huge bed with his crown on his breast. At the foot of the bed knelt six of his daughters, and their wailing mingled with Tserkov's deep voice. He swung an incense burner on a chain. Chanting, he asked God to accept Leo into the brotherhood of monks, and Nevsky saw that the court barber had shaved off the tsar's princely lock. At Leo's right hand knelt Tsarevna Katrina, and behind her stood Ikar Napravo in his grey robes. Elena knelt to the tsar's left, and behind her stood Ivan Levsha, in brown. Leo's foremen huddled in two groups of three, each group eyeing the other with mistrust.

Nevsky looked at Elena. She wore a brown dress with grey brocade, and her eyes were swollen and red. In all his years of visiting Goroth, he had rarely been in the same room with her. True, she attended the New Year Mass, but she never joined Leo for the feasting afterward. Years of sitting in the tower had turned the queen so pale that she looked like a phantom – as pale as her six youngest daughters and the lace they made.

Nevsky leaned over Katrina to kiss Leo's damp brow. The tsar's cheeks were sunken, and his white moustache was limp. Then Katrina, still on her knees, made room for Nevsky.

Leo opened his eyes, blinked as if the canopy of his bed looked strange to him, and said, "So, you still won't kneel to me? Thank God for one honest man!"

He took a wheezy breath and coughed from the incense. "Well, Master Nevsky, you were right." He took another breath. "After the celebrations last night, I disguised myself as a minstrel and visited the nearest manor on the right bank. It belongs to my favourite cousin, who was like a brother to me as a boy, and now he stands somewhere in this room. He may weep, but his household hates me. They even made this toast: 'God keep Ikar Napravo and take the tsar quickly.'"

Looking up, Nevsky caught Ivan sneering at Ikar and guessed that Ikar was sneering back. They were only thirteen, yet they sneered like men.

Leo tried to clutch Nevsky's arm, but the tsar's fingers were losing their strength. "It was the same on the left bank later in the night. I returned from my travels at dawn, but for me the sun was preparing to set. The physicians say I've taken a chill, but I know better. I've sent them away." When he tried to laugh, tears rolled down his cheeks. The crown shook on his breast. "All those years I was foolishly happy, and now I'm dying of grief!"

"Sire," Nevsky said, pressing Leo's hand, "you've renounced worldly goods to become a monk before you die – as all noble men should. Why do you still clutch your crown? Give it away, finally. Undo all of this. Face God with a clear conscience and empty hands."

Ikar stiffened. Ivan scowled.

While Nevsky helped Leo sit up in bed, Elena and Katrina rose to prop pillows behind him. The tsar raised his crown with a shaking hand. With the other hand, he stroked the sable trim and jewelled cross. Ikar and Ivan licked their lips. The scraggly beards sprouting on their chins made them look so devilish that Nevsky wondered how Leo could ever have thought that they were his sons.

"Katrina Lvovna," Leo said, "I name you Queen of Mir. I appoint Master Nevsky as your only foreman, your foremost boyar, and —"

The princes both shouted, "No! It's mine!"

Ikar grabbed the crown before it could touch Katrina's head. Elena screamed. Ivan also lunged for the crown. They tugged this way and that till Nevsky cried:

"Stop this silly tug-of-war! Isn't it enough you're tearing the kingdom in half?"

At the mention of war, Leo's foremen joined the struggle. Each group cursed the other and drowned out the princesses' cries. Only Nevsky saw what Sovah was preparing to do when he unfurled his wings. He swooped at the bed, grasped the jewelled cross in his beak, and wrenched the crown from the princes' hands. He flew back to the beam even as they drew their swords and candlelight flashed from the blades.

Tserkov stopped chanting. "How dare you?" he cried. "Is this how you act? Drawing swords over your dying father? For shame!"

All this time, Starik had stood just inside the door. "Keep chanting, Bishop," he said. "Leave the affairs of court to men of the court."

The princes growled in agreement.

Leo pointed at the door. "Go," he said. "Take your henchmen with you." Muttering threats at one another, Ikar and Ivan made to leave with their swords in hand, with their followers in tow. They stopped when Leo said, "Wait." They turned when he added, "Hear me first." Then he plucked at Nevsky's sleeve and asked, "Will you carry out my final wish?"

"Only if it's wise," Nevsky said.

Trying to chuckle, Leo asked, "Can't you agree with me, even now?" Then he tried to raise his voice so it could carry throughout the room, but his voice grew weak while he spoke. This was why, even as everyone strained to listen, few of them took him seriously.

"Crowning Katrina or one of her brothers won't keep this kingdom together," he said. "Let Ikar rule the right bank and Ivan rule the left. Neither will be tsar until one kneels to pledge his loyalty to the other. But if both of them remain stubborn, then they'll die princes."

When Leo paused to breathe, death rattled in his chest. "Pride made me foolish and, later, blindly happy. What real joy is there when a man laughs with his eyes closed? Master Nevsky, you alone will keep my crown, and you alone will decide whose head it will grace. Burn the bridges connecting Goroth to the rest of Mir. Let these fires be a signal to the people to mourn not only for their tsar but also for their land. And one last thing." He gestured for Nevsky to bend and whispered in his ear.

Nevsky steadied Leo with one arm behind his shoulders. Starik crept forward, and so did Tserkov, but all they heard was, "Don't let them bury me in the crypt. Don't let me become food for worms as my father did. You must –" His voice dropped once more.

Even as Nevsky made sense of what he heard, he shook his head with dismay. At last, though, he nodded and said, "I promise."

Leo turned to Elena. "Can you ever forgive me?" he asked.

Her lips parted. Nevsky had never heard her speak, and he never would. Before she could utter a sound, Leo's eyes glazed and he slumped in Nevsky's arms.

Nevsky closed the tsar's eyes. "He sees as little in death as he did in life," he thought. But he had to say something more fitting than this. Taking up his staff, which he had leaned beside the bed, he straightened slowly and declared, "It is finished – for now."

Chanting once more, Tserkov swung the incense burner over Leo's body. Ikar and Ivan sheathed their swords with a slither of sharpened steel. When they left the chamber, Starik followed, whispering. The foremen also left. The six youngest princesses keened while they crowded about Leo to cover his hands with kisses and tears.

Katrina remained silent and dry-eyed. Nevsky saw that she was now as old as Pavel had been on that fateful day, thirteen years ago. The princess and the boyar should have been married, but Leo had given no thought to her happiness. Had Katrina been a man, he would have praised her to the skies and crowned her. Now the kingdom had no ruler, and the crown belonged to someone who had no use for it. Nor any need. Nevsky pulled Elena from the bed and led her from the chamber while Katrina remained to comfort her sisters and Tserkov remained to chant.

Out in the corridor, even as Nevsky tried to rejoin Pavel and Preestav, he found his way blocked – by Starik. Behind the scribe stood the princes, and behind them lurked their foremen and warriors.

"We will arrange our father's funeral," Ikar said. "Nikolai Starik remembers the old ways."

The scribe told Elena, "You must change into your wedding dress. You will be buried with the tsar and his servants and his favourite horse – in a mound that will overlook the gorge. Then we shall feast. Seize them!"

Warriors grabbed Pavel and Preestav from behind and pressed blades to their throats.

No one touched Nevsky or the queen. "Release them!" he ordered.

Tserkov led Katrina from the chamber. Then he gasped, "For the love of God!"

"God no longer cares for Mir," Starik said. "This was the way of our grandfathers. The way of real men. Leo's household must die with him. The head no longer thinks, so now the heart must be stopped." He threw himself at Elena and gripped her throat, his fingers stained with ink the colour of royal blood. "I'll kill her myself!" he said.

"No!" Katrina cried.

Tserkov moved to help Elena but Nevsky waved him off. When the bishop asked, "Are you going to stand there and watch her die in some pagan ritual?" Nevsky said nothing.

Laughing with triumph, Starik squeezed Elena's

throat till she gasped and fell to her knees. Only then did Nevsky point his staff at the scribe and chant, *"Rahnee menya ee umreeh!* Wound me and die!"

Torches flickered, and Starik released Elena. His hands took on a life of their own. They clutched his throat and threw him against a wall. "S-stop!" he gurgled. Each time his head struck the wall, the icon above him shook. "Let me go!" His face turned as blue as ink, but his hands still clutched his throat. At last, his mouth opened to reveal a swollen purple tongue, and he slid to the floor.

Nevsky pointed at the warriors holding Pavel and Preestav. "Cut their throats," he said, "and you cut your own."

The warriors exchanged glances of disbelief. Then they looked at Starik's lifeless face and dropped their swords. Pavel helped Elena to a chair, and she sat weeping with fright. Preestav shook like a willow.

"Listen to me," Nevsky said. "The tsar may have been foolish and proud, but he never meant to harm Mir. Even you," he told the princes, "are not completely evil. The blood of Dhiavol may run in your veins, but so does Elena's. Renounce Leo's crown, and I will let you live in the palace."

Ikar spat on the floor. "I ask no one for what's mine!" he said.

Ivan snarled, "Nor do I!" He waved at Starik's

corpse. "You can't frighten a prince with simple tricks!"

"Then clear the palace," Nevsky said. He waved his staff at the princes, their foremen, and the warriors. "Go, and take your henchmen – your assassins – with you! My Lord Virnik, my Lord Preestav, come with me!"

In no time at all, it seemed, Oleg was ringing the cathedral bell. It summoned the men of Goroth, who came running while buttoning their coats. Merchants and craftsmen, a thousand strong, milled about in the square. Only two nights before, on this very spot, they had gathered with their families to cheer Leo and the princes after the New Year Mass. "What's happening?" the men asked one another.

"Didn't you hear? The tsar is dead. Ikar Tsarevich has been crowned –"

"No, no! Ivan Tsarevich is –"

"I heard Leo crowned Katrina," a woman said.

Both men scoffed: "Never!"

The sun was touching the mountaintops in the west and lighting the cathedral's cross. The copper domes licked the sky as if they were tongues of fire. After Pavel and Preestav appeared on the palace balcony, Nevsky took his place between them, where the tsar should have been. With his left hand, he held his staff; on his right shoulder, Sovah perched with the crown in his beak. While waiting for the crowd to fall silent, Nevsky shook his head at what he saw.

The men of Goroth prided themselves on working in forges and shops instead of trudging through fields, yet they looked softer and less at peace with themselves than the peasants of Mir. Soon, though, the men of Goroth would learn to love the land. Leo had said this and had added, "It's the only way."

When Nevsky raised his staff, the crowd fell silent. "People of Mir," he called out, "the tsar is dead. But Leo left you no ruler. I am now Keeper of the Crown, as you can see. Most of you wear a grey or a brown feather. Each of you has your favourite prince, but a few have yet to choose." While he spoke, he felt himself growing angry with these men, and with Leo and, most of all, with himself. "Had I been a truly wise man," he thought, "I would have foreseen what would happen." Yet this was no time to be laying blame. He had a duty to fulfill. "Choose now!" he shouted. "In an hour, the bridges will be burned and this island will belong to the church. You must all leave Goroth."

"What?" a man yelled. "He's mad! I've heard of him. He bewitched Leo Dherevo!"

"Why should we listen to you?" another man

yelled. "Are we goats to be herded into the country-side?"

"I carry out the tsar's last wish," Nevsky said. When no one moved, he yelled, "All right, then, see for yourselves!"

And so the men ran for the river. Guards had piled wood under both bridges and waited, torches in hand, on the ice. Seeing this, the men of Goroth lost their heads. Had Starik been alive, he would have written, "Courage is slow, yet fear sprouts wings." Families packed whatever they could into bundles and boxes. With few animals on the island, husbands and fathers harnessed themselves to carts. Merchants filled sacks with jewellery, pewter, and silverware. Looters fought over abandoned goods. Slowly, Goroth emptied. Boyars crossed by the bridges and forced the common folk to cross on the ice. Two lines of carts creaked across the river – until the ice began to crack.

People dropped their belongings and ran for their lives. Men elbowed one another into gaping holes while mothers lost children who fled the wrong way. No one was drowned, no one was trampled under-foot, but the worst was yet to come. Sagging under the weight of boyar wealth, the east bridge collapsed. Horses plunged to the ice and into the water. Riders fell onto carts. Horses whinnied and men cursed, ice cracked and groaned, and women and children wept.

"There has to be a better way," Preestav told Nevsky.

"Does it make you sad?" Nevsky asked. "Good. Does it make you angry? Even better. This is just the beginning, my lords. Let's go down. Here's what else we must do."

Pavel and Preestav listened, and their blood ran cold.

Before the hour was out, only the royal family stood in the square. Ikar, Katrina, and three of her sisters stood together. Ivan, Elena, and her other three daughters stood facing them. Looking down from the balcony once more, Nevsky thought, "How tiny they all seem. Like puppets dressed for a play."

Now Pavel and Preestav joined the figures in the square. Pavel went down on one knee in front of Katrina. "I will live on the right bank," he said. "Not to serve Ikar Napravo but to serve you as I served your father." She touched the golden dagger on his neck chain to show her thanks, and he rose. Nevsky thought she might embrace him, but she did not.

After Preestav pledged himself to serve Elena, Ivan shook his fist at Ikar. "When we meet next, Brother," Ivan growled, "you will kneel to me and kiss the brown feather."

"Or you the grey," Ikar snarled.

With this, the princes turned on their heels and led what remained of their family toward opposite banks of the river. Ikar led Katrina and the others across the west bridge to the right bank. Ivan led Elena and the others across the ice but well away from the fallen east bridge. They stepped carefully so that no more ice would crack. At last, two halves of what had once been a family faced each other from opposite banks. The Reekah had truly become a long mirror.

Nevsky raised his staff. The guards fired the west bridge and what remained of the east. Then the guards ran for the opposite banks. Only Nevsky, Tserkov, and his servants remained to watch while the monks chanted in their House of Song. Two lines of fire burned across the Reekah. Two pillars of smoke rose to form black clouds. The sun had finally set. The sky in the east was indigo, the sky in the west still glowed, and if fire and smoke were not portent enough, the old moon rose in the new moon's arms.

"Take the crown to safety," Nevsky said.

After Sovah flew from the palace to the cathedral steps, Tserkov descended to the square. He wore his heavy robes and mitre and clutched his gold crozier. Nevsky called down for him to stay back, then ran downstairs. He took a torch from a bracket, stepped over Starik's body, and entered Leo's chamber. The hundred candles had burned down, and the tsar lay with his hands crossed on his breast.

"So, Leo the Tree," Nevsky said, "even you have been felled. You died a monk, but I heard no one call you Brother Leo. Shaving your royal lock won't save your soul. It's in God's hands now, but you've certainly chosen to impress Him with your arrival." With this, Nevsky set fire to the bed. Flames climbed the curtains till the canopy looked like a blazing crown.

He fled the room. He ran up the tower stairs and into Elena's chamber. Eight large bobbins for making lace stood in front of eight chairs. Eight bolts of lace lined the walls. He waved his torch in a circle, and the lace caught fire. One by one, he threw the bobbins into the flames. Then he ran downstairs. He ran through corridors and knocked every torch out of its bracket. Flames spread along the floor. In the throne room, he set fire to the dusty animal heads. He pulled down torches and threw them under the throne. Guards had piled kindling at each pillar, and he thrust his torch into the bundles of wood. Standing in the doorway, he watched the throne room burn. Stuffed heads fell from the walls, and the double-headed falcon fell for one last time. Pillars began to groan. Even as he leapt back into the corridor, the pillars collapsed, and the ceiling crashed to the floor.

Tserkov met Nevsky at the palace gates. The bishop looked outraged. "Was this Leo's last wish?" he demanded. "To burn the whole town?"

"Only the palace," Nevsky replied.

He and Tserkov stood at the iron gates and watched the flames reach the balcony. It fell in pieces that rained the courtyard with sparks. Pigeons fled their roosts even as the flames climbed; even as three fires burned in and beyond Goroth. The tower burned as a pillar of flame. The bridges burned like the wings of a fiery bird. And three clouds of smoke joined above the island to blot out the brightening stars.

Shivering with cold and awe, the people of Goroth sang for their salvation, but a different song came from upriver. The peasants of the forest gathered on the banks of the Reekah. Somehow, they knew what was happening. They sang not for themselves as the townspeople did but for their tsar. A cold wind carried the song downriver to Goroth and, from here, a hot wind carried smoke and songs out over the steppes. When the tower fell, it sent sparks so high that they shone like stars: false stars that made no pictures; stars that fell to hiss on the snow.

Tserkov drew back from the gates. He retreated to

the cathedral steps and crossed himself. Red light flickered from his robes. "Is it not enough that you perform pagan rites?" he called out. "Must you also burn the House of God?"

Nevsky signalled for patience, then approached Leo's immense funeral pyre. He stood close enough to touch the glowing, iron gates – so close that the heat singed his beard. Then he raised his staff with both hands and brought the end crashing down. The island trembled. Three times he struck the ground, and three times the land shook from the mountains in the east to the mountains in the west; from Uroth Gorah to the gorge. Then, groaning and creaking, the southern tip of Goroth broke loose. It cracked the ice while floating downstream, and the farther the palace floated, the higher it blazed. The roaring of flames, the smell of burning wood and melting gold, the stench of charred flesh – it looked, sounded, and smelled like the end of the world.

Now a song began downriver. While the peasants of the steppes watched the pyre float past them like a high-prowed ship, they sang of their hope for their tsar: that his final journey would be as rewarding as it was spectacular.

Nevsky sat on the cathedral steps and watched the red sparkle that had once been a palace. After he bowed his head and sighed, Sovah dropped the crown in his lap.

Fingering the crown, Nevsky wondered whether it might fit his own head; whether he and not Pavel might one day marry Katrina and rule by her side. But when Nevsky laughed at this fancy, Sovah eyed him as if warning, "You must be doubly careful." Nodding, Nevsky said, "Call him Leo the Lucky now. But who will write this, and for whom will it be written? Neither he nor his scribe will see what happens next."

When Tserkov asked, "Do you know?" Nevsky shrugged wearily. He watched the sparkle grow smaller till it vanished.

With a loud hiss, Leo's pyre fell into the gorge. Even as the timbers of his once great palace swirled their way to the sea, he faced God with shaven head and empty hands, and how could God not show His mercy? Leo joined the ranks of the fallen, who feast through endless nights, and even now he eats and drinks and likes to boast — as do most dead kings — of his long and glorious reign.

CHAPTER 9:
EKHO'S CHOICE

NOTHING THAT CAME TO PASS IN GOROTH touched life on Uroth Gorah, because Nevsky would not allow it. True, he spent many hours writing out lists of spells, which he then burned in the clay stove, but when it came time for Ekho's lessons or for their walks, he forgot his duty as Keeper of the Crown.

In the days leading up to Easter, just before Ekho's fourteenth birthday, he taught her both the old and new ways of marking the arrival of spring. He knew that Tserkov would not approve, but the bishop had no power here. Nevsky built a fire of cedar logs in the meadow and told her to jump over them. At first she refused, for though the flames burned low, she feared their crackle and snap.

Sovah dove through them with a long, "Hoot!"

"You see?" Nevsky said. "Not one feather singed. We'll do it together."

Hand in hand, they jumped back and forth over the logs. Medvyedeetsa, who had emerged from her den with her new cubs, came to watch. So did Volcheetsa with her new cubs. So did all the other creatures of the forest: the birds and squirrels and deer. Laughing, Nevsky and Ekho landed on their hands and knees in the melting snow. Then the animals began leaping the flames, and soon the meadow resounded with growls and yelps and chirps.

"What does it mean?" Ekho asked. She and Nevsky sat in their home and watched the goings-on. They laughed while the bear cubs and wolf cubs raced one another from the cave to the falls.

"The fire purifies us for the time of no snow," he said. "This is the season for planting crops and breeding cattle. Only those humans and animals who jump through the flames will have a happy year. Those who can't, won't. Now, you tell me the story of Christ's death and rebirth." While she spoke, he searched behind their few books. Her favourite was a copy that Tserkov had sent her: *The Virgin Mary's Journey Through the Inferno.* At last, Nevsky found a cross he had carved from the heartwood of a fallen tree. After Ekho finished telling him the story of Easter, he asked, "Why are there three bars on the cross of our faith?"

She touched the longest one, in the middle. "On this, Christ's arms were tied and His hands nailed down." She touched the shorter bar, above, and traced four letters. "On this the soldiers wrote 'INRI,' which means Jesus of Nazareth, King of the Jews." Then she touched the lowest bar. "This one is tilted because on it rested His feet. See how He pressed one side down in agony?"

Nodding, Nevsky put the cross away. When he turned, he saw Ekho gazing at the staff, which leaned against the wall under a simple wooden icon of the Virgin and Child.

"Master," she asked, "how long will it take me to learn everything you know?"

"You don't have to learn everything I know," he said. "You'll be happier if you don't. Besides, haven't you learned enough? You can read and write. Most old men can't. You can sing, though you didn't learn that from me."

"Soon the eggs will hatch," she said, forgetting the staff. "I'll climb the trees again to sing with the young birds. Shall we eat now?"

He nodded. After she turned to the stove, he took his staff farther into the cave and leaned it against a stone pillar, which grew near the curtain he had hung to hide the door.

Humming while she worked, she made millet

gruel. She sliced rye bread on a wooden platter and poured kvass into pewter goblets. After taking down the honey pot, she said, "It's almost empty. Will you be seeing the beekeeper again?"

"Perhaps." The beekeeper lived in a village downstream from Dherevnia but on the right bank. He kept bees in hollow trees and collected their honey. He was the only person in the forest, apart from Ekho, whom the bees would not sting; but like all the other villagers, he feared Uroth Domah.

Nevsky watched Ekho's long chestnut hair sway while she worked. A silver comb gathered it at the back of her neck. With the birth of his sons, Leo had thought himself the luckiest father in Mir, but Nevsky knew that Ekho had always been the dearest child.

"She's not a child," Sovah said. Perched on the headboard of her bed, he was speaking the language she did not understand.

Feeling a pang of sadness, Nevsky told Sovah, "Too true." He chuckled over sounding like an owl, but Sovah remained serious while he continued:

"If misfortune hadn't befallen Mir, a boyar would long ago have asked for her hand for his son. I've heard people speak of the Maiden of Uroth Gorah, whom they see when she stands at the top of the falls. And because they've only seen her from a distance, they fancy that she's the loveliest maiden in Mir."

"I'll keep it that way," Nevsky said. "No one will get close enough to see how right their fancies are." He joined Ekho at the table. When she asked what he and Sovah were discussing, Nevsky said, "When you stand at the top of the falls, be careful."

She nodded while passing him the bread.

But Sovah was not finished. He hopped to a cupboard beside the stove. "She can't live here forever," he said. "After Mir is reunited, you should present her at court."

"Why think about it now?" Nevsky asked.

"Because," Sovah began and then stopped. Out in the meadow, the animals were scattering toward the trees while birds chirped in alarm. "Look who's coming," he said.

A man had appeared at the top of the falls. He entered the meadow fearlessly, for he was so set on his task that the cave no longer frightened him. He looked thinner than he had for some time, grey hair streaked his brown beard, but Nevsky recognized Boolochnik at once.

They met near the fire. "What brings you up my hill?" Nevsky asked. "You seemed glad enough to leave, last time."

When the baker snatched off his felt hat and strode

past, Nevsky shrugged and followed. Boolochnik stopped in the mouth of the cave, and while he stared at Ekho, she stared back at him with wonder. Besides Oleg, who had barely noticed her, Boolochnik was the first stranger she had met. He cleared his throat and said over his shoulder, "I've come to take her home, Master Nevsky. I want my daughter back."

Nevsky said nothing. Nor did he invite the baker to sit.

Clutching his hat as if it might give him courage, Boolochnik spoke to Ekho. "He's probably never told you, but he's not your father. I am. My name is Petya Ivanovich. My poor Marya Petrovna was your mother, though she forgot you long ago. He cast a spell on her shortly after you were born – to ease her mind, he said, and I believed him. She died last night." He asked Nevsky without turning, "Did you know she had died?"

"Sovah told me." Nevsky entered the cave and once more took his place at the table. He looked at his food but did not feel hungry. Something fluttered in his stomach: something – or someone – he had thought would never return.

Boolochnik told Nevsky, "That owl sees everything!" The baker looked angry enough to spit. "Then you also know that Marya left me a boy, finally, after all these years? I can't raise him alone.

The girl must return to help me."

"Hah!" Nevsky began to eat, then threw down his spoon. The gruel had gone cold, and his stomach was twisting into knots. "There are plenty of widows who will sell themselves into your service to buy land for their sons," he said. "You could even marry one, and she'll kiss your feet. If all you want is a servant —"

"That isn't all!" Boolochnik cried. "I miss her."

Nevsky's heart hardened. He recalled the day he had saved Ekho — the day the people of Dherevnia had rewarded him with blows and chased him through the forest. "He misses you," he told her. "Yes, he's your father. I never said that I was. But did he visit you once in all these years?" Nevsky glared at the baker. "You don't even know her name. You left her out to freeze without having her christened."

"Yes," Boolochnik told her. "I did." He began to brush dirt from his sarafan. "And it's true I don't know your name." When he threw his hat on the table and grasped her arm, she screamed.

Nevsky leapt to his feet. Sovah hooted, and she heard, "Don't be afraid." Then she wondered why Sovah had said this and not her master. He looked as if he was far away, as he so often looked these days. He was pressing with his fingertips at the scar on the left side of his brow.

"They made me cast you out," Boolochnik cried.

"Like a burnt loaf. The butcher and the milkmaid and all the rest. Even Father Sashenik, who calls himself a priest!" Tears filled the baker's eyes. "You were the most beautiful baby born in Dherevnia. That's why the Evil One came for you. Can't you see that I loved you?"

"But who saved her?" Nevsky asked. He could feel the scar reddening – felt his brow begin to throb – so he raked his fingertips back through his hair.

Still holding Ekho's arm, Boolochnik wiped his eyes with the back of his free hand. "All right, he saved your soul. I couldn't. But he didn't want you at first. Ask him what he said when I begged him to take you in."

"I said," Nevsky told her, "'Sovah is the only friend I need.' That's not true. It hasn't been true since that first night, when this man who calls himself your father left you and ran away. I raised her, Petya Ivanovich. Which of us loved her more?"

Ekho shook free of the baker and ran to the back of the cave. She wanted to hide behind the curtain, behind the door itself if she could. She wanted to escape these men who quarrelled over her like precious wax. Biting her lip, she dabbed tears from her eyes with a corner of her apron. She had never heard voices raised in anger. Why now, so soon before her birthday? Why now, on the first day of spring?

Nevsky sat down once more. "Ekho?" he called.

"Ekho," Boolochnik whispered. "A strange name."

"It is, and I gave it to her. What did you ever do for her?"

Boolochnik siezed a loaf from the table. "I bake the very bread she eats!" He told her, "I bake it! He used to come in the night like a bear and I would give him food for you. I gave him clothes your mother sewed with cloth she wove and thread she spun herself, though she never saw you wear them. But before she died, his spell wore off. She remembered you, at long last. She died crying that she would gladly face the Evil One again if she could save you from this madman! I've heard of him. He's famous for his wit. He counselled the tsar, and see where the tsar is now! Come home," Boolochnik pleaded. "This Nevsky-Dhurak can offer you nothing. Come live in a cabin instead of this hole. Eat meat instead of gruel. Play with real children like your baby brother instead of with animals!"

"I'm not a child," she said. She turned to face him without leaving the back of the cave. He stood with his arms stretched out to welcome her. Nevsky sat with his back to her and his head bowed. "Two men quarrelling," she thought, "but my master has never made me cry." Looking at Sovah, still perched on the cupboard, she asked, "What should I do?"

"Why ask me?" he replied. To Boolochnik, it sounded like nothing more than a hoot. "The choice is yours alone."

"Look at this," the baker told Nevsky. "She's going mad like you. Haven't you done enough?"

Ekho dried the last of her tears with her apron, then brushed her tears off the cloth. She removed her comb and ran her fingers through her long hair. Sovah had told her how Nevsky had traded his gifts from court: a silver belt for a silver comb; high black boots for this apron; a golden pin for the slippers she wore on holy days. She straightened her light green dress and put the comb back in her hair. "My place is where I am now," she said. "Where I shall always be."

Boolochnik scowled. "You'll change your mind soon enough. Why, even last year, the church would have let you marry, but whom would you have married? This madman who hasn't a flock of goats to his name? Why should he marry his servant?"

She shook her head at all these harsh words. "When Master Nevsky and I return from our walks," she said, "he sits down and I draw off his boots. Sovah tells me that no servant does this for a man if he has a daughter. Or a wife." She stood behind Nevsky's chair and placed a hand on his shoulder. "For now I do it as your daughter," she told him. "But, one day, I will do it as your wife."

Nevsky looked up in disbelief. He rose and took her hand. She truly had grown. Gone was the childish wonder in her hazel eyes. He looked from them to Sovah's all-seeing eyes and then he scolded himself. If only he had never entered this cave. If only he had not grown up overnight. She was a mere ten years younger than he, yet the wisdom of ages separated them. How could she be happy with a wise man who spent his days muttering useless spells? At once, though, he changed his mind. "I do love her more than anything," he told himself. "Even more than the land."

He did not hear Boolochnik stamp away. The baker turned to curse them and saw Medvyedeetsa seated by the fire. She glowered at him while licking her chops. With his heart in his mouth, he scrambled downhill and back to Dherevnia.

In Uroth Domah, Nevsky watched a breeze ruffle Ekho's chestnut hair. It was glinting like copper among sunbeams; like the domes of a cathedral; like a gilded cross. Her eyes shone like stars to soften the heart he still hardened against so many men. "If only everyone could be like her," he thought. "Then Mir would be a land of peace once more." And though he felt that it was wrong – that he could never make her truly happy – he took her in his arms.

Soon laughter rolled down Uroth Gorah, and the rainbow appeared ever so faintly in the mist. Then the laughter set birds to flight and warmed the heart of every creature in the forest. Somehow, they all knew what had happened.

"I love you, Ekho," Nevsky whispered, and he kissed her.

"And I love you, Master," she said. "With all my heart. When will we be married?"

"As soon as bridges span the Reekah once more," he said.

"That long?"

"It won't be long, I promise. I'll take you to Goroth, finally, and the bishop himself will marry us in his cathedral. It will be the happiest day of my life."

Laughing and crying, from joy this time, Ekho kissed Nevsky's face and hands. He twirled her in the cave while Sovah circled the meadow. "It's true!" he called. "It's true!" He called till the animals and birds returned to follow him, once again, through and over the flames. They growled and yelped and chirped once more – to mark not only the return of spring and Resurrection of Christ but also the blossoming of love.

CHAPTER 10:
GOD OF FIERY SKY, GOD OF THUNDER AND BATTLE

NEVSKY AND EKHO HAD NEVER BEEN happier, but all their love could not save Mir from the dark days that soon befell the land. Snow melted from Uroth Gorah, the mountain turned purple and green, but in the rest of the kingdom, winter lasted into spring. The rainbow danced in the falls, yet the Reekah remained frozen. Weeks dragged by, and snow fell on the forest and the steppes. Sovah flew the skies at dawn and dusk and returned to tell Nevsky everything. Village priests, who had closed their churches, sacrificed roosters to sacred oaks. Old men and warriors danced in masks that were carved like animal heads.

The people of the right bank called the sun Dazhbog and asked him to shine brightly to melt the snow. They called the wind Striborg and asked him to blow warm air to chase away the cold. On the highest hill of the right bank, Ikar Napravo raised idols carved from cedar that greyed overnight. Each morning, when the sun tinted the snow on the slope pink, he climbed alone to pray to Svarog, the god of fiery sky.

Ivan Levsha prayed to even older gods. He worshipped Pieroon, god of thunder and battle, god of storms and war. His men searched far and wide for stones that had been struck by lightning, for pieces from Pieroon's hammer. Standing in the ring of stones on the highest hill of the left bank, Ivan's priests wailed and moaned. They sacrificed goats to Mokosh, the goddess of water, and begged her to stop choking the Reekah with ice. Sculptors carved a dog from a pine tree and painted it brown. Every morning, Ivan led his priests, Father Sashenik among them, in prayer. When the sun rose, the priests chanted to the dog: "O, Semur, run through the forest and across the steppe. Spread the seeds of life over us, so that life may spring once more from the earth."

At first, Nevsky laughed when Sovah told him all this. Soon, though, his anger grew. One day, he left in a fury to meet Pavel, as he did from time to time, at the foot of the falls.

Nevsky ran down the steep, muddy path. Then

he pulled on his wolfskin cloak when he reached the bottom, for it was much colder here than on Uroth Gorah. He forgot his fury when he saw how cheerful the young boyar looked. Pavel brought gifts from Katrina – her cast-off clothing, this time – for Ekho. But when he, too, told Nevsky what went on in the houses of the right bank, Nevsky muttered, "Fools! They think God's turning His back on them, so they turn their backs on Him."

"It's not the people's fault," Pavel said. "They follow the princes and their councils."

"Hah! If only they thought for themselves, they might suffer less. Thank you for your gifts."

A smile brightened Pavel's face while he fingered his flaxen moustache. "No," he said, "thank you for your hope."

Peering over the bundle to see his way, Nevsky climbed the hill. The path was frozen near the bottom, but near the top it turned to mud. By the time he reached the meadow, he felt so warm that he had to pull off his cloak. Then he caught his breath. "I've heard so many spells," he thought. "Not one of them promises hope, yet how can I say this to Lord Virnik?"

Spring finally arrived – on Midsummer's Day. Instead of celebrating a late Easter Mass and chanting, "Christ is risen!" the priests bowed to their idols. People hung skirts on birch trees and danced around them. At his shrine on the right bank, Ikar sacrificed a grey foal to Dazhbog as thanks for melting the snow. On the left bank, sculptors carved a wooden bull, painted it brown, hung juniper from its horns, and called it Velesh, the giver of cattle and wealth.

That same day, Sovah brought an invitation from Tserkov for Nevsky to visit the cathedral. The bishop was planning a special evening Mass, but Nevsky refused to attend. He worried about Ekho and made her stay close to home. "I don't want you stumbling across villagers foraging in the hills," he warned. "They might carry you off and sell you into slavery."

"They won't," she said. "They're too weak."

Only then did he learn that Sovah was telling her what went on in the forest and on the steppes. In all of Mir, only she wept for the people, while she stood at the top of the falls. Through Sovah's eyes, she watched the people watching the sun. "They're like feeble insects now," she thought. "No more or less than ants scurrying about their hills." But even ants had feelings, and she knew that these creatures, whom Nevsky scorned, were sick at heart. Sometimes she wanted to leave him so that she could help them. How, she did not know; only that Uroth Domah felt too comfortable now. True, she often lit the cave with splinters of wood instead of with candles, but she served their food on pewter, and they never lacked for honey.

While Ekho and Sovah wandered close to home, Nevsky sat staring into flames in the stove. Before the times of trouble, he had gone beyond the door once a year, always upon returning from Goroth after the princes' birthday. Now he went more often. He returned with his beard singed and his clothes bloodied, and yet he found little more than the same old evil in that other world. It held nothing good or new that might help him in this one. Only when Ekho was close to him did he feel content. He delighted in touching her hair, stroking her face, and listening to her songs.

One day she asked, "Will we be married soon?"

They were spending the morning under an oak while birds sang in the branches. Nevsky was pacing with his head bent and his hands clasped behind his back. He stopped and said, "First I must save Mir. I told you: bridges must span the Reekah once more. Only then can we expect true happiness."

She leaned against the broad trunk and smiled up at the birds. "But how will you save it?" she asked. She looked lovely in a sleeveless white dress that Pavel had brought from Katrina. The princess herself had mended the tears.

"I don't know," Nevsky said. He took up his staff and traced lines among the tree's thick roots, which snaked in and out of the earth. "These are the people who still have hope," he thought. "A princess and her lover, a wise man and his love, a bishop, and an owl. Five people and a bird can't save a kingdom!" Then he looked into Ekho's wondering eyes and smiled. "Sometimes I don't care," he said. He set the staff aside, lay down, and let her cradle his head in her lap. At first he stared at the sun through the branches. Then he closed his eyes and said, "Sing me a song."

Curling his locks about her fingers, she sang. Uroth Gorah became a garden and the valley, which the snow and ice had left at last – the valley seemed to melt like his cares.

Soon, though, the people of Mir wished that this strangely late spring would end. Teeth broke from wooden plows, and the steppes spat out seeds. Termites burrowed through cabin floors, and fleas bit babies while they slept. Even the boyars were not safe in their country homes. Lice infested their clothes, and no matter how often the boyars steamed themselves in bathhouses, no matter how often they lashed themselves with reeds, their skin crawled across their flesh. In the old days, boyars had never fasted to prepare for Easter, when the common folk had eaten only fish. Now there was not even fish to be caught. Nothing swam in the river. Horses, stolen for their meat, vanished from stables, and the people still prayed to their gods.

When summer came, hard on the heels of spring, the people began praying for autumn. Rats infested the villages, crowded now with the merchants and craftsmen of Goroth. Plague felled people in the streets. Then the spirits of the dead feasted on the flesh of the living and so the plague spread. Corpses were burned, not buried, and the ashes scattered in the fields.

One night, the streams and wells of the right bank went dry. And as if the Reekah was a wall that reached to the sky, clouds rained only on the left bank.

Ikar refused to swallow his pride. He sacrificed a colt to Striborg, the wind, and begged him to blow the clouds across the Reekah. The colt's blood soaked the ground in vain. Every crop withered, and one day Ikar called his council together. It met in the hall of an old foreman, Leo's favourite cousin – the very hall that the tsar had visited in a minstrel's disguise.

Pavel remained with Katrina outside the hall. Warriors were blocking their way because the princess was forbidden to attend.

Leo's cousin sat at one end of a long oak table.

Ikar sat at the other end. While boyars spoke in circles, the old foreman listened. At last he rose on shaking legs.

"In my youth," he said, "the Reekah overflowed its right bank but not its left. Why, no one knows. It destroyed our crops and drowned our cattle. The people of the left bank shared their grain with us. No one feasted that year, but no one starved."

The boyars, led by the other two foremen, muttered into their cups. Pavel told Nevsky later, "What galls them is not that their people starve but that the people of the left bank eat."

Pulling his chain of loyalty out from behind his beard, the foreman hobbled to the far end of the table. "Ikar Napravo," he said, "no one loved your father more than I. We played together as boys. Didn't I stand in his chamber and weep even as he died? Now he cries to us from beyond the gorge. I beg you to end this madness. Let your brother be king. What does it matter? Our people must not starve."

"Treason," a boyar grumbled. "The hunger has emptied his head."

The foreman fell to his knees in front of Ikar and clutched the hem of the prince's grey robe. "Boyars will always have enough to eat," he said. "So will warriors. But our people have nothing! Is it treason to kiss the cross before your brother does? Do we not call you Napravo, on the right?"

Ikar's lips curled back from his teeth. Then, closing his yellow eyes, he said, "Execute this traitor."

Before the foreman could cry out, younger men pulled him onto the table. The warriors outside opened the door to watch even as the boyars drew their swords; to laugh while they hacked him to death. Katrina screamed. Pavel pushed past the warriors and stood in the hall with his own sword unsheathed.

"The wise man's spy," a boyar growled. Having smelled blood, which made him feel brave, he wanted more.

Ikar held him back. "Well, my Lord Virnik," he said, "have you come to collect the bloodwite from me?"

"No, sire," Pavel replied. "I've come to collect it from your council. The law says that if more than one man raised his sword, all of them must pay." He glared at the prince and thought, "How easy it would be to kill him."

"My Lord Virnik demands payment," Ikar said. "Pay him."

For a moment, Pavel thought that the boyars would fall on him, as well, but they pelted him with coins. Gold clinked against the wall and rolled across the floor. He sheathed his sword, collected the coins, and placed all but one in his purse. He tossed this one coin to Ikar. "Your share, sire," he said. Then he left the hall to give the old man's widow the rest of the bloodwite.

That evening, Sovah glimpsed a chaika crossing the river. Ikar stood in the stern of the small boat while four warriors rowed. A storm was raging over the left bank. After mooring near a village, the warriors waited for the storm to reach its peak. Then they crept ashore. They tied torches to the horns of cattle and goaded the cattle into setting barns on fire. The lowing of the cattle and thundering of Pieroon's hammer caused a din. Thinking an army was attacking, villagers fled to their fields. The warriors loaded grain onto the chaika, and even as they pushed off, Sovah flew quietly above them. But before he could teach them a lesson, lightning struck the chaika and it capsized. Precious food floated downstream. The warriors could save nothing, for their weapons pulled them under. Sovah screeched at Ikar while the prince dragged himself, soaked to the skin, onto the right bank.

Ivan and his court laughed for days.

Vowing revenge for this laughter, Ikar sacrificed a gelding to Svarog, the god of fiery sky. Autumn came, and the people of the right bank harvested what little they could. They stared longingly at the grain rippling in the wind on the left bank.

When the harvest moon rose, Ivan Levsha hung garlands of fruit on the horns of Velesh, the giver of cattle and wealth. The clearing near the shrine resounded with music while his people danced.

They awoke the next morning to a frightful buzz. A greenish-yellow cloud was approaching the left bank. It was a cloud of locusts. Terrified, the people ran for shelter. Cowering in their cabins, they stuffed cracks with rags and burned fires to keep the locusts out of the chimneys. The cloud lifted at noon. Unable to believe their eyes, the people staggered into their fields. Not one stalk of wheat remained. Not one stalk of rye. Wells were clogged with the bodies of animals that had tried to escape the locusts, which had stripped cattle to their bones. All summer, Ivan's people had laughed at his brother's subjects. Now they wandered through fields as bare as those on the right bank and wondered what they had done to deserve such a fate.

The harvest moon had set and the hunter's moon barely risen when the winds blew cold again. The people prayed that winter would remain a long way off, but they could not stop the seasons from changing any more than they could stop bodies from rotting in the sun. Autumn's faint beauty went unnoticed – except by madmen and hares. Striborg, the wind, blew icy blasts from the north to cover Mir with snow. Mokosh, the goddess of water, fled to warmer skies and so the Reekah froze. Only four months after winter had left, it returned. The people reached their wits' end. Foraging like animals for straw to pound into gruel, peasants lost their way in blizzards, and the steppes became dotted with men frozen in their tracks. Widows sold their children into slavery, for it was better that they should fight for scraps under boyar tables than starve in their mothers' arms.

Christmas and New Year came and went. Easter approached, once again with no sign of spring – this time not even on Uroth Gorah.

Ekho cried bitterly for the people, yet Tserkov suffered for them more. As godless as the people of Goroth had become, he missed them. He ordered his servants and the monks to prepare a meagre celebration for Easter. Then he climbed the bell tower, silent since Leo's death, and here he found Sovah. The bishop removed a sprig of holly from one of his pockets. Sovah had brought the sprig three months before, to mark Christmas. Tserkov fingered the shrivelled berries and brittle leaves and wondered how to bring them back to life. Once red and green, they lay nearly black in his palm.

"Is this all the colour left in our land?" he wondered. "Surely there is more?"

He looked north over Goroth with its empty houses and empty streets. No soot sullied the snow on the rooftops because no smoke rose from chimneys, and yet he missed the sight of ash settling on snow. The townspeople had left much food, which had lasted nearly a year, and only now did Olga add dried goosefoot leaves to flour when she made bread.

He turned to look south. The island ended in a crescent as if a monster had taken a huge bite and swallowed the palace whole. Shading his eyes against the sun, he searched the land. Behind him, the forest and orchards were brown; in front of him, the steppes were grey.

"No, there is no more," he thought. "Mir has truly been drained of colour." And yet he was mistaken – because, at this very moment, a woman shouted, "God is great!"

Tserkov looked across the frozen river. Women stood on the right bank and waved to him. They wore red shawls. With his heart pounding, he turned to see women on the left bank, as well. They wore green skirts. Children appeared, and before long a hundred women and children stood on the banks of the Reekah. The people had been forbidden to set foot on Goroth, and so these women and children stared longingly at the House of God.

"Come!" he called, waving to them. "Come back to Mother Church!"

No one moved until a woman glanced over her shoulder, then ran down the snow-covered bank and onto the ice. Others followed her. Hearing their shouts of joy, the women on the opposite bank also began crossing the river. While children tottered or rolled down the slope, Tserkov thought he heard a sound he had not heard since Leo's death. He thought he heard laughter.

"God still lives in women's hearts," he told Sovah. "The sanctuary will be full for Easter, after all."

"Who," Sovah said.

To Tserkov, it sounded like, "Don't be too sure."

Almost at once, he heard an eerie whistle followed by a thunk, then more whistles and thunks. He tried not to cringe, but he could not help himself. The bell tower bristled with arrows, and their feathers – some grey, others brown – quivered in the sun. The women stopped running because warriors had appeared. Some aimed their arrows at the bell tower, but most aimed their arrows at the children.

"So," Tserkov exclaimed, "the princes guessed their people might try to find comfort in my cathedral! They still fear me, it seems." Then he shouted,

"Go back! Save your children for tomorrow. You've shown me what I must do!"

With their shoulders drooping, the women and children turned their backs on Goroth. They returned across the ice and let the warriors herd them like goats out of sight.

Looking north once more, Tserkov squinted for a glimpse of Byelleeye Falls. "Why should I wait for our friend?" he asked Sovah. "I'll act myself."

"Who?" Sovah asked.

To Tserkov, it sounded like, "You?"

"Oleg!" the bishop called. Waving the sprig of dried holly, he hobbled down the stairs. "Dress yourself! I want you to carry a message. Two messages. It's time for this madness to end!"

The next morning, while the sun filled Mir with a cold yellowish light, two young men approached Goroth from the right and left banks of the Reekah. They wore high wolfskin hats above wolfskin cloaks trimmed with marten's fur. The bitter wind flapped their cloaks open to reveal dull robes and, as always, Ikar wore grey while Ivan wore brown.

Waiting in the town square, Tserkov noticed that the hem of his gold robes showed from under his black cloak. He wondered if this might be a sign — yet another reminder that Mir had not been drained of colour, after all. He tapped his crozier on the ground while muttering the words he planned to say.

Sovah watched from an arm of the cross on the highest copper dome.

Ikar and Ivan stopped, facing one another.

The grey prince spoke first. "You should thank me, Brother," Ikar said. "Every day, my boyars urge me to declare war. It's as difficult to hold them back as it is to hold back hounds when a stag is trapped by a cliff."

Ivan laughed, then said, "My warriors stay awake all night hoping you'll slink across the Reekah again. Next time, we won't leave anyone alive for the river to swallow."

When Tserkov raised his crozier, the sunlight flashing off its jewelled crook silenced the princes. "There's a simpler way than war to settle this," he said. "Let Nevsky crown Katrina as tsaritsa. For as Leo himself declared on his deathbed, she is the rightful Queen of Mir."

Ikar snorted. "Then let her sail down the river into exile," he said, "so I don't have to look at her face. Mir no longer exists. Nevsky-Dhurak destroyed it at my father's command." The grey prince waved his right hand at the spot where the palace had stood.

"We agree, for once," Ivan said. "Mir is a phantom kingdom, and its ruler is a phantom queen. After I conquer the right bank, I'll give this land a new name. It will be born out of war, and so I'll call it the Kingdom of Voyna."

"Enough," Tserkov cried. "Must your people keep suffering? Don't you see that God has visited famine and pestilence and death on them? Must you now add war?"

"Hold your tongue, Bishop!" Ivan growled. "Be thankful we've left the bell in its tower and not melted it down for weapons. Why, I don't know, since your flock is small enough: two old servants, and monks no one sees. What good does your bell do our people? They may wail now, but they'll cheer when I kill my brother."

The insult to the church angered Tserkov. He snapped, "Kill each other, then, and be done with it!" He took a deep breath to calm himself before saying the words that had troubled him all night: "Why not fight a duel?"

Ikar grinned and his nostrils twitched while he slid his sword from its scabbard. Ivan threw back his cloak to free his arms and said, "Yes, now!" Even as he drew his sword, he attacked.

"Stop," Tserkov cried. When he thrust his crozier between the princes, their blades bit into wood. "You must fight between the right and left banks, but not here. Not on sacred ground."

Ikar scowled at the bishop. "Except for this island, every spot in Mir is either on the right bank or the left. Should we fight in mid-air like hawks?"

Tserkov pointed beyond the cathedral. "In the meadow above the falls," he said. "Tomorrow at noon."

Ivan stroked his scraggly beard. "I want no part of the madman!"

"Why not?" Ikar taunted. "It's the perfect spot. Nevsky-Dhurak can crown the victor. He will crown me, at last."

Ivan looked at the sky and Tserkov saw fear in his yellow eyes. "Very well," Ivan said. "I'll bring my boyars to make sure you don't play tricks."

"Then I'll bring my warriors," Ikar said, "so your boyars don't set on me like wolves!"

"And so will I!"

Heading their separate ways, the princes left Goroth.

Tserkov raised his eyes past the four corner towers with their copper domes, then past the bell tower with its central copper dome. Sovah dove from his perch on the cross and landed on the crozier. "God forgive me," the bishop said. "I've rolled a boulder off a cliff, and it will sweep us away."

Staring at the bishop, Sovah said nothing.

"He looks so much like Nevsky," Tserkov

thought. "As if they're one soul divided in two. But this is no time for fanciful reflections." Then he spoke: "Well, my owlish friend, perhaps youth will succeed where old age has failed." He called, "Oleg!" and climbed the cathedral steps. When his servant appeared in the doorway of the southeast tower, Tserkov said, "Ready my sleigh. We leave for Uroth Gorah!"

C H A P T E R I I :
ThE KEY

SOVAH FLEW HOME TO TELL NEVSKY WHAT had taken place in Goroth. Tight-lipped with fury, he waited for Tserkov to arrive. Ekho knew better than to disturb her master at times like this, when he muttered spells that sounded like curses and curses that sounded like spells. He no longer left the pine-tree ladder next to the falls, for he wanted no one from the valley on his hill, and so Oleg helped Tserkov up the slippery path. Planting his crozier in the ground for support, the bishop struggled to reach the meadow before the sun could set. Then, while Oleg carried the gold mitre, Tserkov followed the Neva to Uroth Domah.

Once inside the cave, he stamped his feet, and snow fell from the hem of his robes onto the bearskin rug. He looked about and said, "I see why you no longer visit us, my son. You have everything you need here." He blessed Ekho, who bowed to him in welcome. She was just as Nevsky had described her — lovely and kind — but the bishop noticed something that Nevsky must also have seen but never thought to mention. Like Katrina, whom Tserkov had known from the day of her birth, Ekho had hazel eyes.

All this time, Nevsky had kept tapping a goblet on the table. Now he stopped long enough to say, "You had no right to step in like that."

"It's my land, too," Tserkov said. "What have you done in the past year? How many times have I heard you put Leo's courtiers to shame? And added another grievance to the long list that vulture, Starik, kept. What are you waiting for?"

Passing a hand over his eyes, Nevsky said, "The key to all of this." He felt a soothing touch on his shoulder and looked up to see Ekho standing next to him. With her other hand, she held a jug of hot mead. Waving at the table at last, Nevsky said, "Do sit down. You must be tired. You, too, Oleg."

Tserkov leaned his crozier next to the staff. It no longer intrigued him, as it once had. And, he saw, the scorpions that had once worried him no longer looked like magic symbols. They looked like harmless decorations.

Oleg placed the bishop's mitre on a bench. He sat

facing the fangs in the back of the cave, and though he tried not to look at them, he could not help himself. Beyond the fangs hung a curtain, and he wondered why it did not hang closer to the mouth of the cave – in order to hide the fangs. He fidgeted with a spoon next to his empty bowl.

After Ekho poured mead for the bishop and his servant, Nevsky said, "There has to be a key, but I can't find it."

"Why not?" Tserkov asked. "You're a wise man."

To this, Nevsky snapped, "Even wise men don't have all the answers!" Bored with tapping the goblet, he left it alone and rubbed the backs of his hands.

Ekho spooned gruel into four pewter bowls. When she picked up her own and made to turn away, Nevsky asked, "What's the matter? Are you suddenly shy?" He tried to ignore Sovah, who perched on a cupboard and looked at him as if he had said something foolish.

"Nothing's the matter," she said. Then she faced the table and asked, "Why can't you be as kind to others as you are to me?"

"What!"

She placed her bowl on the table and looked at him boldly. "Only three men have ever visited us," she said, "and you've quarrelled with two of them now. First you scorned my father. Yes, you had reason, but couldn't you have been more kind? Now the bishop visits us, and you raise your voice to him. Master Oleg is the only one I've never heard you quarrel with, but he rarely speaks. You weren't like this in the old days."

"Who?" Sovah asked.

To her, it sounded like, "Not true."

"We're not quarrelling, my child," Tserkov said. "It's just that your master's ways have always puzzled me. It's as though he sees the same stars in the sky as I do, yet the pictures he sees are different. Why should this be, when it's the same sky?" He told Nevsky, "You have so much of your life ahead of you, but I can't wait as long as you can to see the bridges rebuilt."

Nevsky put his arm around Ekho's waist. "I'm sorry," he said. "Come, eat with us. But first, stoke the fire in the stove. Even with their hot mead, our guests must be chilled." While she moved to a willow basket and picked through logs, he told Tserkov, "The sun sets so quickly these days, as if it's glad to leave us." Then he asked kindly, "But why on my land? The most peaceful place in Mir."

"I'm sorry, too," Tserkov said, "but you can't hide in this cave forever. Don't you hear the people crying? Doesn't Sovah tell you what goes on? All I've done is whip the hounds to start the hunt. One of the princes will win the duel and reunite our kingdom."

Without warning, Oleg dropped his spoon and it clattered on the table. Nevsky ignored him. Laughing in Sovah's direction, Nevsky waved at Tserkov. "He thinks the loser's boyars will stand by and watch their prince die." He told the bishop, "You've arranged a battle, not a duel. Yes, Sovah sees everything. More than I ever have. Noon tomorrow, you say? By sunset, bodies will cover Uroth Gorah. The snow will be redder than the sun is now. Blood will fall from the Neva into the Reekah, not melting snow. Don't you see?"

Tserkov did not see. His eyes glistened while he looked through Nevsky as if he was not there. The bishop saw only Ekho, who sang softly at the stove. Whose chestnut hair glinted like Katrina's red hair, like fiery copper domes.

And Oleg no longer fidgeted with his spoon.

Nevsky looked at Sovah, then at Ekho. When he raised a finger to his lips, she looked surprised, but she stopped singing. "What are you thinking of now?" Nevsky asked Tserkov.

"War."

"And a moment ago?"

"Of how this place smells so much like my cathedral, and yet no beeswax or incense burns here. I thought I saw the icon screen above the royal doors, but –" He frowned.

"And you?" Nevsky asked Oleg. "A moment ago?"

"Oh," he said dreamily, "I was thinking of how beautiful the meadow looks. It's so peaceful, so green, and the stream turns pure and white when it falls. And that rainbow!"

"You have your back to the meadow," Nevsky said. "The Neva is covered with ice, and the meadow is knee-deep in snow. Don't you remember plodding through it just now, when you arrived?"

Oleg blinked and looked over his shoulder. Turning to face the back of the cave, he lowered his eyes. "I don't know how, young master," he said, "but I saw it as clearly as on a summer's day."

"And yet you've been here only in winter."

"What are you saying?" Tserkov asked.

"Ekho," Nevsky said, "sing us a sad song."

Still at the stove, she sang about autumn, when leaves wrinkle on trees; when geese fly south and bears go to sleep. Smiles appeared on the faces of both guests. Even as Nevsky watched, Tserkov and Oleg began to shimmer, and the rainbow appeared. It danced over Byelleeye Falls. He closed his hands over his ears, and both men returned. So did the footprints on the meadow, and the evening sky. The rainbow vanished and yet, even after Ekho finished her song, Tserkov's smile lingered, and Oleg looked entranced.

"That's it!" Nevsky cried. His chair fell over when he leapt to his feet. Grasping her shoulders, he said, "To think the answer's been here all along! You are the key."

"To what?" she asked. "What have I done?"

Pacing the length of the cave, he waved his arms and tugged at his beard. Sovah hopped from the cupboard to the table and back to the cupboard. "The boyars' ears are shut to everything but talk of war," Nevsky said. "They can't remember how beautiful their land was. All they see is what they don't have: their enemies' land. I've seen, but I can't reopen their eyes. I've heard, but I can't make them listen." He told Tserkov, "Only Ekho can. That's why Dhiavol wanted her soul!" He was about to scoff at the bishop, who was making the sign of the cross, but thought better of it. Nevsky turned to Ekho and said, "You must sing at noon tomorrow, before the duel begins."

She wiped her hands on her plain green apron. "I can't," she said. "I've never sung for anyone except you and Sovah and the creatures of the forest."

"You sang for me just now," Tserkov said. He

stroked his white beard thoughtfully. "My son, I believe you're right."

"And you sang for me," Oleg added. "You sang so beautifully. Your voice was so warm, so tender..." Tears came to his eyes.

"You're my master's friends," she said. "These boyars and warriors he speaks of are evil."

"They're not," Nevsky said. "They're simply fools. Unholy fools, it's true."

"And the peasants of the forest and the steppes? Aren't they evil, as well, with all their ignorance? Didn't you curse the people of Dherevnia when they drove you out?"

Nevsky gasped, "Who told you about that?"

"Sovah did."

"Who?" Sovah fluttered up from the cupboard and hid among dried fruit that hung from the cave's fangs.

Tserkov and Oleg chuckled.

Taking her hands, Nevsky said, "Even wise men make mistakes. Besides, I was only a boy then, a boy with power he couldn't control. You saved me just as I saved you. My heart softened, and I learned to care for people. To forget they needn't all be wise like Sovah or kind like you."

He faced Tserkov and said, "It's true I don't love the people of Mir. I never will, because I think with my head, while you think with your heart. But I do care for them. In my own way." He faced Ekho once more. "You care for them even more than I do. The boyars will slaughter each other if you don't sing. Then the warriors will carry the battle into the valley, and the people will have to fight or die. Either way, they'll die, but they won't go to heaven. They'll go to Dhiavol and never know peace again. Mir itself will vanish from the face of the Earth."

Turning away, Ekho covered her face with her hands. "I'll lose my voice with all those strangers listening," she said. "I dread even meeting them. All my life I've lived here and never walked the paths of a village or the streets of a town. I believe everything you say, Master, but you have more faith in me than I. You know more than I ever will."

No one spoke then. Nevsky looked at the darkness outside and shivered, but he could not bring himself to draw the curtains closed in the mouth of the cave. "How many times I could have taken her to Goroth," he told himself. "How many times she asked me for the key, and I refused. How much longer can I keep refusing her? And how much more?"

He pulled the necklace out from under his shirt and fingered the iron key that hung between two large pointed teeth. After reaching behind his neck, he untied the cord slowly. Then he led her past the stove and the fangs to the curtain that hid the door. After pulling back the curtain, he unlocked the door and pushed it ajar. First, a mist floated out to swirl across their feet. Next, a hot breeze blew the mist through the cave and out of its mouth. After knotting the cord behind her neck, he pulled her hair through the necklace and let the hair cascade like a silken waterfall down her back. Then he straightened her silver comb.

Tserkov and Oleg were speaking in excited whispers, but Nevsky shut them from his thoughts.

Ekho fingered the teeth of Medvyedeetsa's father but could not bring herself to touch the key. Without turning, she asked Nevsky, "What if I don't learn to sing for others? Our land will surely be doomed."

"That's true," he said. "You might not learn anything beyond this door. Sometimes I've seen nothing. Other times, I've been nearly frightened out of my wits. Once or twice, I wanted to stay. That was the worst. Only my memories of you brought me back. I never told you this." He shook his head sadly. "There's so much I've never told you, my love."

When she turned and hugged him, he felt her tremble. He wanted to go with her, but he knew that she would learn nothing if he went. "Goodbye, Master," she said. She kissed him as if they might never meet again, and he finally saw what he stood to lose: not only the child he had raised as his daughter but also, now, the young woman who would one day become his bride. As for all that she stood to lose – he could not allow himself to think of such things.

He opened the door fully, and she took a step forward, away from him. The mist rose to surround her and grew so thick that she vanished from his sight. The door began to close. Then, at the last moment, he decided that he did not want her to grow up, after all. He wanted her to stay young forever. "No," he shouted. "Come back!" But the door swung shut.

THE
KEEPER
RELENTS

FOR THE SECOND TIME THAT NIGHT, OUR court erupted in a flurry of voices and pounding cups, and one of the ladies at my table cried, "What has he done! They were so happy together!"

"He?" a lord scoffed. "What about she? Silly girl, agreeing to go beyond the door and no doubt throwing away everything they might have shared! If the people in that kingdom are so easily seduced by greed for their brothers' land, they deserve to be damned."

Once more, other courtiers groaned over having been awoken from a vivid dream. This time, the foreign merchants held their tongues though their throats must have been parched. As before, the hounds awoke, but instead of beseeching us for scraps, they contented themselves with being petted by indulgent masters and mistresses.

And here, let me tell you of a strangely wonderful occurrence from the first part of the minstrel's tale that had recurred during the second part. His harp had accompanied him musically, as one might have expected while he had plucked its ten strings, but it had also accompanied him in a manner that one might not have expected. Not even from an instrument that traced its roots to the magical *lyra, cithara,* and *harpa* of bygone days.

The minstrel's instrument was that type of harp known among our court musicians as a frame harp because its three sides do, indeed, create a frame. A sound box rose on a slant from his left knee toward his left shoulder; a forepillar also rose on a slant, but forward; and a slightly bowed neck snaked from the top of the sound box to the top of the forepillar. Where the neck and forepillar joined, there was a finial, and the finial on the minstrel's harp – that singular frame harp he strummed – depicted a dragon's head. I thought this an odd choice of decoration, for he spoke of the dragon in the same breath as he spoke of the devil. But I supposed then, and still do now, that what he valued in that finial was the depth of its chiselled lines.

As for the sound box, because it accounted for the

largest expanse of wood on his instrument, it was admirably suited to embellishment and yet, apart from its three sound holes, the sound box was plain. Rather, it appeared to be plain. During the first part of his story – and again during the second part – I could have sworn that the harp had illustrated his tale.

My daughter scoffs when I speak of such things, but here is what I had seen early on – a cave like an ogre's head, a village in a forest, and a wooden bridge; a cathedral with octagonal towers surmounted by domes, a palace with iron gates; a two-headed falcon, bolts of lace, and a waterfall. During the second part of the tale, I had seen many other images and yet, as before, I had seen no living creature – neither goatherd nor goat, neither bishop nor owl, neither horse nor wolf nor bear. Why this should have been, I could not guess at the time. Nor can I now. But nothing my daughter says can shake my conviction that the minstrel's harp illustrated his tale – much as tincture and leaf illuminate the books in the library that is now mine.

During the second interlude, the minstrel once again appeared unmoved by the uproar in our court. When he reached for his cup, I thought he would raise it for more wine, yet he placed the cup mouth-down next to his chair to signal that he was nearing the end. At this, my betrothed gave me a knowing glance. It combined his regret that we had been denied our tryst in the garden – for it was now long past midnight – with his appreciation of the night's entertainment. For, though the minstrel's tale was a simple one, and though he told it more simply than I would have done had it been mine, it satisfied our need to be transported, however briefly, out of our everyday lives.

And it was typical of our everyday lives at court that a lord should have called to the Keeper of the Queen's Library, "So! The luckless king will have his prince, will he?"

Lords and ladies laughed, some more kindly than others.

The keeper no longer sat with his arms crossed and his eyes closed. Indeed, once the minstrel had begun the second part of his tale, the keeper had not maintained such an attitude for long. He had even chortled when Leo had announced that Elena had borne twins. And now the keeper surprised us by laughing – at himself. "Is it not a good thing we insisted that the minstrel continue?" he asked. "Rather than taking to our beds."

"We insisted?" a lady scoffed.

"I meant, that is, Her Majesty," he said.

All eyes except the minstrel's turned to the gossamer curtain, and we saw that the old queen appeared unwell. She sagged with her left elbow on the arm of her throne and her right hand, with its jewelled ring, clasped to her brow. My beloved fixed me with a look suggesting that the ring might soon be mine; and yet, despite my impatience to replace her on the throne, I could not countenance his look. Indeed, no one felt more heartened than I when she at last responded to a word from her lady-in-waiting.

"Perhaps," the keeper said, "Her Majesty would prefer that the minstrel stopped here for the night?"

I was tempted to ask, "Stopped here in his tale, or stopped here in the palace?" But a jest like this would have been in poor taste with our queen so clearly distressed.

At another question from the lady-in-waiting, the queen gestured as if to say, "It will pass." And, as if to reassure us, she composed herself with her hands in her lap and returned to twisting the ring.

Her lady-in-waiting stepped out from behind the curtain to announce, "It's the late hour, nothing more."

"Before you continue, Minstrel," my betrothed called out, "I should like to hear how my friend, the keeper, would end your tale."

A lady exclaimed, "Oh, yes!"

Courtiers and merchants applauded while the

keeper rose. As for the servants, though they watched him with an ill-disguised amusement that bordered on contempt, they made as little fuss as did the hounds that rested at our feet.

"Very well," he said. "Anyone who can read –"

"And," my beloved declared, "there are a few among us with this gift!"

" – knows what will happen next." The keeper said this loudly through the laughter that had ensued. "Not that I would wager a single book in my keeping on the outcome. For, as Her Majesty herself has said, one good book is worth a hundred silver coins. To which I could add that one bad book is worth its weight in stone." When he faced the curtained dais in hopes of some royal sign of appreciation, the queen tilted her head wearily.

Thus, I commanded him to finish with all due haste.

"Of course, Lady Chancellor," he said. For once, he did not try to remind me – as did so many of his fellows – of his disapproval over my appointment as our queen's right hand.

"Here it is," he announced. "The girl will return to save the kingdom. She and the wise man will marry, then have sons. Many sons. Indeed, if I may be so bold as to embellish my own ending to this tale, I should add that there will be seven sons and one daughter; that each of the sons will have some magical power; and that their sister will have none. But –" Here he wagged an admonishing finger at us. " – it will be through her purity alone that the seven sons can use their power to, perhaps, save yet another kingdom from, let us say, an evil sorcerer."

"Such a gift for endings," a lord called out. "It's our loss that you never learned to write as well as you claim to read!"

Amid the applause that followed, my betrothed asked, "What would you call this new tale of the seven colourful sons and one daughter? Surely it is far too long to be an epilogue to the minstrel's own tale, and so deserves its own illuminations? And its own separate binding."

"Hmm," the keeper said. He looked about while ignoring the smiles of lords and ladies who dared him to disappoint us now. Then his eyes lighted on the curtain, whose gossamer acted as does perfumed oil that is spilled on darkly hued, sunlit stone. "I should call this new tale – *The Rainbow Knights.*"

It now seemed that the court might turn to debating the merits of this title and to asking the keeper to list the powers of the seven sons. To forestall this diversion, I tapped my chain of office, and its clinking conveyed my impatience.

Bowing to the blind old man, the keeper said,

"Minstrel, we are in your hands once more. Take us where you will."

He nodded his thanks and settled his harp on his knee while we prepared ourselves to be transported once again. Yet we did not find ourselves back in that other realm. Rather, like the virginal heroine of his tale — who was about to discover a world less sheltered than her own — we found ourselves far removed from the Kingdom of Mir.

PART THREE:

THE
MASTER,
ONE WHO HAS SEEN

CHAPTER 12:
BEYOND THE DOOR

EKHO'S POUNDING HEART FLUTTERED EACH time she shivered, not from cold but from fear of the unknown. Beyond the door, she knew, there lay a passage; at the end of this passage was another cave; and outside the cave lay another world. "A place only Sovah and I have seen," Nevsky had said. But she could see nothing, neither passage nor cave, and for now she could not imagine a world other than the one she knew.

That world was behind her now. When she turned, she could not even see the door, for the mist swirled about her like a winding sheet.

"Three steps," she thought, "and I'll reach the door. One more step, and I'll be home." Yet she knew she could not face Nevsky if she failed to learn her lesson – whatever it might be. She turned her back on the door and took a deep breath. Fearing to take another step with nothing to guide her, she felt for a wall. She lost her balance at once. Even as she fell against clammy moss, she screamed. Shuddering, she wiped her hands on her apron. After this, she walked with her arms outstretched, for it was better to graze the invisible walls with her fingertips than to fall against the moss. "If only I could hear something," she thought. But when she scraped her feet along the passage floor, the noise died even as it reached her ears.

After an age, she heard the thrip-thrip of water dripping in a cave, and she quickened her step. This was when something fluttered behind her. She crouched, too late, and wings brushed her hair. She shrieked, but the noise died once more. Then she wondered whether she truly had screamed. She must have, for her throat felt dry. Flapping its wings, the creature flew on as if daring her to follow. Once again, she thought of turning back, and once again she went on. After a while, she began to hum.

A light appeared almost at once. It was so faint that she thought she must be mistaken until it brightened. The passage grew so wide that she could no longer feel its walls. The mist thinned, and she found herself standing in a cave. Sovah had told her that people found Uroth Domah frightening, but she could never imagine why. It always looked welcoming to her after her walks. It made her feel safe. This cave was not even as interesting as hers. There were no fangs in the back of its mouth. It was nothing but a cave, and yet it would lead her into a world that she hoped would be much like her own.

She blinked in the dazzle of light. The sun had set when she had left Mir, but the sun was rising in this land. The sky was growing light in the east, and what she saw made her shiver – again, not with cold but with fear.

In her own land, the indigo sky of night turned blue by day. This sky was orange. Worse, the rising sun glowed a bright green. While the sun of Mir rose, it changed from red to orange to yellow, but this sun changed from green to blue to purple. She felt as though someone had turned her upside down and inside out. And that she might go mad.

At her feet, an orange brook trickled across a red meadow and vanished over a cliff. This much seemed the same as home, so she followed the stream. She felt strange walking on red grass, and yet it felt as soft beneath her shoes as the grass of Mir. She stopped to look over her shoulder. Light blue trees with red crowns lined both sides of the meadow. Higher up the slope, behind the cave, red and yellow pines pointed at the orange sky. They looked impossible to climb. "I'll do it after I'm used to these backward colours," she told herself.

Then she wondered, "How long must I stay? My master wants me back by noon. It's dawn here, but I couldn't have been walking all night! And what if I'm not ready to go back? I'll be of no help to anyone." She clapped her hands once, loudly, to give herself courage. She was about to say, "I'll return when I'm ready," but the words stuck in her throat. Her hands had turned a bluish black.

She stared at them for a long time as if they were not hers; as if she had not only entered a strange world but also changed into someone awful. Then she gathered a handful of hair and slowly pulled it over her shoulder. Her once white gown looked black, and her once chestnut hair looked light blue. Tears filled her eyes. She hated this world because it made her feel ashamed. "Am I learning a lesson," she wondered, "or being punished?" Then she straightened her back, clapped her hands once more, and followed the stream to the falls.

Below her lay a kingdom much like home, but no mountains ringed this land. The hill on which she stood was the only high ground in sight. The orange stream turned black while it fell onto white rocks below, then returned to orange and flowed toward a crimson lake. She had never seen a lake, but she knew what it was called. "Lakes have bounds," Nevsky had told her once, "but oceans and seas? They have no bounds. They flow into one another and back again, so that our world is not so much a collection of lands as it is a gigantic sea dotted by far-flung islands. Some are tiny. Others are huge."

She had not asked him how he knew all this. She had had no need, for she always believed what he said. Now, though, she wondered whether she should. The question worried her so much that she returned to looking out over this strange new land.

On the near shore of the lake stood a town. Its high towers were the only real buildings in sight. True, she could see villages, one of them near the foot of these falls, but they were nothing more than huts thatched with purple straw. Farms of different colours surrounded the villages. All the land had been cleared, so trees grew only on this hill. It was late summer here, not late winter as in Mir, and fields of wheat shimmered under the purple sun. Row after row of silver spikes arced in the wind while other fields, recently planted, looked a flat red.

Soon her eyes grew tired of all these warm colours: red fields, an orange sky, a yellow forest on the hill. She longed for the cool colours of home: green, blue, and purple. This kingdom did not look as peaceful to her eyes as did her own. "But then," she reminded herself, "we have no peace in Mir."

She picked her way carefully down a path to the bottom of the hill. Here she followed the path between golden birches to the village she had seen. The huts were built of grey stone, and none of them had a rooster painted over the door. "Perhaps the people here aren't afraid of fire," she thought.

The huts ringed a green well, and here an old woman in a white gown stared at her over a light blue bucket. The woman's skin was a wrinkled bluish black.

"Greetings, Old Mother," Ekho said. "Where are all the people?"

"At the trial," she replied. "They leave me to work, as always. I'm to dig my own grave, I suppose, after I die?"

"Whose trial?" Ekho asked.

"The Painter's. In the town, where you should be." When the woman dropped the bucket, it fell for a while and then splashed. Tugging on the dark blue rope, she grunted, and with each tug she smacked her toothless gums.

Ekho touched the sides of the well. It was made of long green blocks that felt rough. "What is this?" she asked.

The woman stopped long enough to reply, "Brick." She muttered to herself while pulling the bucket into sight, "What is this? Heh!" She poured water into a blue clay jar and heaved it onto her left hip. Years of carrying the jar had bent her to the right. She looked as if she spent her days peeking around corners – to ensure the coast was clear.

"Let me help you," Ekho said.

"Strangers only muddy our water," the woman snapped. "Like the Painter."

Her words stung, and yet they whetted Ekho's curiosity, and she decided to attend the trial. After bidding the woman farewell, Ekho set off for the town on the edge of the lake.

The road did not wind like the forest paths of Mir. There were no surprises awaiting her at the next turn, no rises or dips. The road ran straight and true. "But how true?" she wondered. Nor were there goats in the fields or birds in the sky. Only once, far away, did she see a white cow grazing in a red field. For the first time since having arrived here – for the first time in her life – she felt lonely.

Soon, though, she wished she was alone.

She made this wish the moment she entered the town. People acted as if they were at a fair, not a trial. Jugglers juggled, tumblers tumbled, musicians played, and everywhere she looked she saw coins changing hands. Sweetsellers passed their trays close to children's noses so that the children would cry for sweets. Innkeepers openly mixed water with their drink, but men gladly threw back their heads to guzzle the emerald wine.

"Surely Goroth was never like this?" she wondered. Though she had never visited the town, she knew of it from Sovah. Life here seemed more harsh than life had been in Goroth, while the buildings seemed less welcoming. They had not been lovingly made from wooden planks and beams, then carved with designs taken from the land. These buildings had been pieced together from grey stone or the rough green brick, and not a single shutter or door had been decorated with carvings.

She wove her way through the jostling crowds, and though she had thought that she might be afraid to be among so many people, they fascinated her even as they repelled her. Even their clothes were strange. Instead of woollen sarafans, the men wore blue leather jerkins, and their boots were also blue. Maidens wore black gowns like hers while all other women wore white. Only the children wore clothes of different colours, but even the children worried her, because they pointed at her and laughed.

Only now did she notice that all the women wore scarves while her own head was bare. "My master says it doesn't matter what people think of us," she told herself, but he was not here to say this again. She did not like being laughed at, and so she stopped at a clothseller's booth and asked to hold a green kerchief. It had not been embroidered, but it would nicely set off her apron, which looked red here.

"One silver piece," the man said.

"But I have no coins!" she cried.

"Then give me something in exchange." He stooped over the counter, pushed his face close to hers, and leered. "One kiss from you is worth a silver coin, I'll wager."

She drew back, and not only because he smelled of the watery wine. She felt as if she was on sale and not the cloth.

"Too plain for you?" he asked. "Jewellery then."

"I have nothing that God or my master didn't give me," she said, "and I can't part with my silver comb. Wait, though. I can sing! I'll trade you a song for the kerchief."

His leer vanished. Looking both ways, he hissed, "Are you mad? Take this and hold your tongue!" He crumpled the kerchief into a ball and closed her hands about it.

"Don't you want to hear me sing?" she asked.

"Certainly.not!" His eyes darted like an animal's that smells a trap. "You know the law. No one sings alone here."

Before she could ask him why, a crowd swept her

toward the castle. Somehow, amid all the jostling, she unfurled the kerchief and tied it onto her head.

Surrounded by a moat that was choked with red scum, the castle's white walls towered over the marketplace. Soldiers paced on the drawbridge, and a spiked grate, waiting to impale someone, hung beyond the moat. The soldiers wore red shirts under blue jerkins. Their leggings were black, and their boots were dark blue. She nearly laughed because they looked like children dressed for play. Even their light blue pikes, with their sharpened iron points of orange-white, looked harmless.

Once in the castle courtyard, the crowd fell silent. It broke up, and the people formed new rows behind other common folk. Shutting her ears to curses from women as well as from men, she slipped into the front row.

The common folk stood on three sides of a courtyard as large as a meadow. On the fourth side, to the right of where she stood, rose a royal box hung with yellow banners. In this box sat a king and a queen in olive robes trimmed with black fur. Behind them in tiered rows of boxed seats sat noblemen and ladies, and at the king's right hand sat a man as lean as a pikestaff. He wore white robes and a silver chain.

"He must be the judge," Ekho thought. She

dared ask no one about him, so she looked at the entertainment.

In the middle of the courtyard, white-skinned men in black loincloths danced in a circle around a lone man who was taller than the rest. Slashing at him with curved swords, they closed in and backed away so quickly that their blades blurred. Meanwhile, a band of other white-skinned men played a tune on flutes, drums, and bells. The tune was so garish — so foreign to her ears — that she thought it would take her forever to learn.

Now the tallest dancer, the one who was trapped in the middle, began leaping into the air. He leapt so quickly that his feet barely touched the earth, but the other dancers came so close that he had to leap high to avoid their blades. At last, they gave a shrill cry, rushed the middle, and sliced their blades downward. He should have been cut to bits; yet he leapt over their heads. He turned a somersault in mid-air and landed in front of the king. The music stopped. The people cheered while the lords and ladies clapped politely, and the queen tossed coins to the dancers. Then, led by the musicians, they withdrew.

"The Painter!" a voice called.

After a moment, others took up the cry. "Bring out the Painter! It's noon."

Ekho looked up. The purple sun shone directly

above the courtyard to cast shadows that were short in the harsh light. "Did I spend all morning walking here?" she wondered. "Time flies too quickly in this land. It can't be noon at home."

When the king raised his hand, the people fell silent. The lean man rose and called, "Raise the scaffold!"

Ropes creaked and chains clanked while hatches slid back to reveal a square hole in the middle of the courtyard. Then more ropes creaked and more chains clanked while a blue wooden scaffold rose into sight. After the hatches slid forward to cover the hole, soldiers began tossing bundles of light blue sticks under the platform. Before long, the entire space bristled with wood that could only be meant for burning. Two soldiers leaned a short ladder against the scaffold and then withdrew.

"Bring out the prisoner!" the man in white robes ordered.

A heavy door swung open near the royal box. Out marched two jailers, one on either side of a man who was blindfolded with a white cloth. He was almost as tall as the leaping dancer. Unlike the jailers, whose skin was bluish black, this man's skin was a light blue: here, the colour of wood. His ankles and wrists were shackled with white iron chains that clanked at every step. He wore a long loose shirt that was not belted over his trousers. And unlike everyone else's clothes, his had been embroidered – with silky black thread on the black cloth.

The jailers marched him to the scaffold. With one behind him and one ahead, they pushed and pulled him up the ladder. A few of the common folk shouted insults, but most remained silent, for he kept his head high. Even in the rough hands of his jailers, he seemed to be at peace. They shackled his left ankle to a ring set on the platform and only then unshackled his hands. As if afraid he might harm them, or as if afraid of the sun itself, the men backed quickly down the ladder and into the darkness of their jail.

The prisoner removed his blindfold and threw it into the air. The cloth turned into a black dove, but no one oohed or aahed. The dove flew over the castle wall and out of sight. Swinging his arms now, to and fro in large arcs, he circled to look at the crowd. Even as he finally faced Ekho, she gasped.

"It can't be!" she cried. When people stared at her, she lowered her eyes and whispered, "Your pardon." Then she thought, "I left my master behind."

Looking up again, she saw that this man could not be Nevsky, after all. The prisoner had no beard, and his nose was hooked. Strangest of all were his eyes. Everyone here had red or orange eyes that looked forever hateful, but his had no colour. They shimmered like water in a well. She felt as if she was staring down two long tunnels. Worse yet, and worst of all, she felt as if he was willing her to join him on the scaffold.

She knew – as surely as if he had told her – that if she did not close her own eyes, his would pull her from the crowd. They were kind eyes, yes, but they were eyes that could break a young woman's heart; eyes that could lead her, if she did not take care, to her doom.

CHAPTER 13:
"LET THE DUEL BEGIN!"

THE BOOMING OF DRUMS ALONG THE REEKAH rolled through the forest, up the slopes, and echoed from mountain to mountain. Horns blared, loud and shrill, while animals and birds fled.

By mid-morning, long columns marched along the banks of the river. One column was grey and the other was brown. At the head of each rode a prince, boyars, and a warrior bearing a flag. Behind them came more warriors on horses, and behind them marched footmen – the men of Goroth. Villagers watched while the armies passed with their eyes fixed on Uroth Gorah. The footmen prayed to Svarog, the god of fiery sky, or to Pieroon, god of thunder and battle. So did the men of the countryside, who had not yet taken up arms, but the women and children prayed to God.

Nevsky prayed to no one. He stood at the top of

Byelleeye Falls and wondered what had become of Sovah. He had vanished the evening before, and Nevsky had paced in the meadow while Tserkov and Oleg slept fitfully. And while pacing, Nevsky had recited every spell he knew. He had changed the order of the words, changed the tone of his voice, yet nothing promised hope. His shoulders drooped while he watched the armies' approach. "I can't save Mir now," he thought. "Only Ekho can."

From the top of the falls, the armies looked like serpents. Each had a colourful head, but the serpent on the right bank had a grey body while the serpent on the left bank had a body that was brown. Slithering toward Uroth Gorah, they grew darker at bends in the road, where footmen trod on one another's heels, and lighter when the road straightened. Then there was the noise: the blare of horns and boom of drums. When the armies neared Byelleeye Falls, pillars of ice broke off to shatter on the frozen river. Only now did the horns fall silent, and only now did Nevsky realize that each army sang the same song:

Beat the drum!
Beat the drum!
Then sound the battle cry.
Victors come!
Victors come!

Their weapons held on high!
Lay down your weapons now,
And crawl like worms in mud.
Too late to beg forgiveness now.
Too late, you'll pay with blood.
Find in our victory,
Honour in slavery.
Kiss our prince's hand.
We'll show you mercy still,
Yoke you to plows to till
What's ours by right: your land!

They don't hear.
They don't hear.
Now sound the horn and drum.
Smell their fear.
Smell their fear.
They know their end has come.
Rejoice, rejoice, rejoice!
Tonight a king and kingdom will –
A kingdom will be born!

The serpents began to climb Uroth Gorah. Instead of rearing their heads gracefully and sliding uphill, they broke into pieces that shouted and cursed while clambering up steep paths on either side of the falls.

Nevsky could not imagine how the boyars' horses could make the climb till he saw whip marks on the rump of Ikar's grey horse. The prince had cut into its flesh with his crop, and Nevsky saw the pain in its eyes. He turned away when the horse whinnied for help. He returned to Uroth Domah.

After Tserkov pulled back the curtains in the mouth of the cave, he gave the traditional Easter greeting: "Christ is risen!"

Instead of replying, "In truth, risen," Nevsky asked, "Are you so sure?"

The bishop squinted at the sun. The air was so cold that when he sighed, ice formed on his beard. He said, "A hard battle they fight once more – frost and the sun. Here it is the beginning of spring, and still your Neva hasn't begun to melt. What if it doesn't melt this year? What if winter lasts forever?"

"I don't know!" Nevsky said. He tore a leather pouch off a hook on the wall. The scar on his brow throbbed.

Oleg, who had been sleeping on a bench, opened his eyes with a startled grunt.

"I don't know," Nevsky repeated more kindly. He tried not to scowl at the servant, who rose to help himself to gruel from a pot on the stove. "How things change," Nevsky thought. "Guests sit at my table and the one I love is far away." He looked at Ekho's holy day apron, which hung beside her linen cloak.

Also looking at the apron, Tserkov asked, "She still hasn't returned?"

"No, and when she does, she won't be the Ekho we knew."

"Why? Will evil befall her? What if she can't return?"

"She will!" Nevsky opened the leather pouch to look at Leo's crown. "All this madness," he thought, "for a cap of leather and sable and a jewelled cross." He tied the pouch to his belt. "Have faith in my strange ways a little longer," he said. He dashed cold water onto his eyes, which were red from lack of sleep. Then he took up his staff and strode from the cave. He climbed on top of Uroth Domah and stood next to the chimney. From here, he watched the two armies claiming his meadow as their battlefield.

The princes wore gold helmets and breastplates. Bearskin cloaks fell from their shoulders to their saddles and flowed back toward their horses' tails. Across the saddles lay long two-handed swords with scalloped blades. The boyars wore silver helmets and breastplates under wolfskin cloaks, and their scabbards slapped against their horses' sides. The warriors did not wear cloaks. They wore iron breastplates over sheepskin coats, and their helmets were shaped like the cathedral's domes. Each warrior bore a short bow dangling from one shoulder and a quiver of arrows from the other. Last came the footmen, dressed in wool and wearing no armour. Ikar Napravo's men carried their axes over the right shoulder, and Ivan Levsha's men carried their axes over the left. Boots and hooves trampled crocuses that were trying to poke their shoots through what should have been melting snow. Now, no spot in Mir was untouched by hate.

Tsarevna Katrina and three of her sisters had come with Ikar. Tsaritsa Elena and her other three daughters had come with Ivan. The seven daughters of Leo met in front of the cave and embraced. All except Katrina dabbed at their eyes with their lace kerchiefs. Then the queen and the princesses bowed to Tserkov.

He wore his mitre and held his crozier, and though it was cold he did not wear his cloak. He wanted the sun to glint not only off the armour but also off his golden robes. He looked almost happy while he blessed the women.

Elena wore black, and deep lines of mourning creased her face. Nevsky knew that she had not smiled since Leo's death, but even when alive, he had rarely given her a reason to smile. Katrina also rarely smiled, but her eyes held hope. Neither Leo's refusal to crown her nor her brothers' birth – nothing had shaken her faith that one day she would be the Queen of Mir.

Pavel stood behind Katrina, and Preestav stood behind Elena. Of all the boyars, only these two did not wear armour. True, they bore swords – one to protect Katrina, the other to protect Elena – but Nevsky had not seen Pavel's sword unsheathed since that fateful day in the throne room. Glancing up, Pavel nodded at Nevsky and then looked for the Maiden of Uroth Gorah, about whom he had heard many fanciful tales. Nevsky nodded back. After all these years, Pavel still looked youthful, and just as Katrina's hair glowed red in the sun, his hair and beard shone like flax.

Elena and Katrina sat on chairs in front of Uroth Domah, and the six younger princesses sat on a bench. Tserkov, Pavel, and Preestav stood behind the women while Oleg, ever the servant, fussed with dishes in the cave.

Standing alone on top, Nevsky looked at the battlefield. The armies had formed lines on either side of the meadow, Ikar's on the right and Ivan's on the left. The horses snorted vapours into the air. Boyars and flag-bearers gathered in knots in front of the warriors and footmen. The trumpeters and drummers stood, facing one another, at the far end of the meadow, at the very top of the falls. In one motion, Ikar and Ivan dismounted. Had Nevsky not been furious with this whole foolish play, he would have laughed over the princes' trying to look ferocious; trying not to trip over their long, two-handed swords. Such weapons should have been far too heavy for such young men, yet Ikar and Ivan bore them as lightly as quill pens.

After Nevsky opened the pouch at his belt, all eyes turned to him. Sunlight glinted off the jewels on the crown when he waved it like a plaything. "My lords," he called. "Look at the crown Leo Dherevo entrusted to me. Would you spill your blood for a fancy cap?"

"No more words, Madman!" Ikar shouted. "It's time for deeds. Let real men decide who will be king!"

Nevsky scowled. When he tapped his staff on the roof of Uroth Domah, the cave chuckled. "Real men?" he asked. "Real men know when to fight and when to make peace. Years ago, I used a spell against my worst enemy. Tell me what it means." He did not chant the words, as he had to Dhiavol. He spoke each line and waited for it to roll out across the meadow:

> Stab me and cry,
> Wound me and die,
> For only one of us is true,
> While the other is a lie!

"Simple," Ivan said. "Only one of us is the true heir of our father's crown. The other is an impostor who must be killed."

"And which of you is the rightful tsar?" Nevsky asked.

Both princes shouted, "I!"

He scoffed and put away the crown. He felt so tired from lack of sleep that his fingers fumbled with the drawstring of the pouch. Finished, he saw that the sun shone straight down. He could no longer wait for Ekho's return.

"My lords," he declared, "drown the valley with blood if you must, but don't stain my land. Advance and fight in the Neva. Let it carry your blood over the falls and into the Reekah. Your precious blood."

Ikar and Ivan cringed, but they dared not lose face in front of their men. The princes left the safety of their armies to stand in the stream. The thin ice cracked, but for now it held their weight. Hoping that the grinning cave would frighten his brother, Ikar stood with his back to Nevsky, but Ivan saw only the pouch. Nevsky raised his staff and held it motionless. Horns blared and drums rolled. He plunged the staff between his feet, and the cave rumbled. He struck the roof twice more and only then called, "Let the duel begin!"

Howling like wolves, the princes attacked. Even as they advanced, they broke through the ice. Water filled their boots, stones made footing treacherous, yet the princes felt nothing. Growling taunts, they swung their swords in long arcs and brought them crashing down. Ikar pressed his brother at once. Unable to raise his sword fully, Ivan defended himself with short sideways strokes. Then Ivan screamed so fiercely that Ikar halted. Now Ivan attacked. Ikar stumbled backward against jagged ice and fell against the Neva's right bank. Laughing while he raised his sword at last, Ivan brought it whistling down. But the blade glanced off the bank, for Ikar had rolled to one side.

Men in grey cheered while men in brown groaned.

Back and forth, the princes duelled. The longer they fought, the more slowly they moved – till each motion took an age. Everyone saw that they were so evenly matched, neither prince could win. Boyars on both sides rattled their swords in their scabbards. Warriors beat the ground with their bows. Footmen shifted their axes from shoulder to shoulder and spat in the snow. One by one, boyars drew their swords to examine the sharpened blades.

Even Nevsky could not say which army advanced first. Before he could stop them, the

eldest foreman on each side pointed his sword at his reflection. With one voice, they yelled, "Forward!" Horns blared and drums rolled while boyars, warriors, and footmen advanced. The battle for Mir had begun.

C H A P T E R 1 4 :
ThE TRIAL

IN THE LAND OF BACKWARD COLOURS, THE TRIAL had also begun. The judge straightened his white robes, rattled his chain of office, and called out, "Prisoner!"

Ekho sighed when the Painter's eyes released hers. He faced the royal box squarely, so that she could see only the right side of his face. Now more than ever, with his hooked nose, he resembled a hawk. Without raising his voice as the judge had, the Painter said, "I do have a name."

The judge laughed drily. "So do we all, but people address persons of rank by their titles. I am My Lord Justice. The king is Your Majesty. Since you also hold a special place in our land, though not in our hearts as does our king, you must also have a title. You may call yourself a painter, but you are his esteemed Prisoner."

The Painter shrugged.

"Prisoner," the judge said, "you are charged with treason. During the past three years, you have criss-crossed our land. You have painted portraits of noble men and women, of merchants and their wives, of –"

The Painter interrupted with a laugh. "Yes, My Lord Justice. I painted the warts on their noses and the lines around their eyes. They didn't pay me for that! But then, if they'd wanted to see themselves as they really were, I suppose they could have simply looked into mirrors. Oh, my poor fools! You're afraid to see your true selves, and so you charge me with treason. That's a crime that covers everything in this land from inciting rebellion to criticizing the cut of the queen's robes."

When people began muttering at his manner, Ekho saw why he reminded her of Nevsky. "They have that same mixture of compassion and arro-gance," she thought. "How can such men survive?"

"I will tell you why you've been charged," the judge shouted. "You need not tell me! When artists offered to pay you for lessons, you took them on as apprentices. Generous man! Yet you taught them to use the wrong colours. You taught them to paint our kingdom with green fields –"

The people gasped.

"And blue skies –"

The people shrieked with laughter.

"And yellow suns. You mocked the very symbol of our king!"

"Treason!" the people yelled.

"Why, Prisoner?" the judge asked.

"Because that's how I see field and sky and sun," the Painter said. "I paint what I see, My Lord Justice, not what others see. I see that you, for instance, wear black robes, not white. Robes as black as your heart. Any of my apprentices can tell you this." He looked at the crowd and nodded, yet no one nodded back. "I see two right there, behind that moneylender. Ask them to paint for you."

Now the king laughed, then straightened his silver crown. "Yes, they're all here," he said. "All twelve of them. They begged my forgiveness and I granted it. I am once more their master. But you? You are master of nothing and no one. You are alone."

The Painter looked at his light blue hands. "I see," he said softly, yet his despair passed quickly. He raised his head and again turned in a circle to his left. While he searched for the rest of his apprentices, his eyes flicked past Ekho, then returned as if he recognized her. Once again, she felt him willing her to step from the crowd, and she braced herself against the pull. She sighed with relief when his eyes moved on, and he faced the judge once more.

The judge smiled and said, "Don't despair. Our king in his wisdom has given you one last chance. Renounce your twisted ways, and His Majesty will make you his court painter. Refuse, and you will be burned as a mere prisoner."

"You would still execute me one day," the Painter said. "The day I painted the cruel pinch of your mouth, My Lord Justice. And, Your Majesty, the ignorance in your cowardly eyes."

The king leapt to his feet with his hands clenched. People cursed the Painter and surged forward, but soldiers held them back. The judge ordered more soldiers off the battlements and into the courtyard. Before long, armed men stood every five paces in front of the crowd.

"Bring out the canvas!" the judge ordered.

One of the jailers brought a rectangular board covered on one side with stiff black cloth and tossed it up onto the scaffold. The other jailer brought paints and brushes, which he also tossed up, then rubbed his hands with distaste.

Both men hurried back to the jail.

The Painter gathered his paints and put them near the canvas. He ran loving fingers across the brushes and blew dust from their hairs. He softened stiff bristles by whisking them in a cupped palm.

"Look up, Prisoner!" the judge ordered. "Behind me rises the ivory tower of His Majesty's castle. Beyond that is a clear orange sky, and in its midst shines the royal purple sun."

"Paint what you see," the king said.

The Painter laughed with scorn. "Your subjects might just as well be born blind," he told the king, "since you tell them the colour of everything around them! Should I paint what I see, or what My Lord Justice tells me to see?"

"Do as you wish," the king said. "Only remember that you stand between punishment and reward. Between death and life."

Nodding, the Painter sank to his knees. He blew dust off a corner of the platform and began to mix his paints. Then he looked up. Ekho wished she could watch him work, but he stood above her as if on a stage. Once in a while, he stopped painting and squinted at the sky or the tower. Once, he even stared into the sun and had to wipe tears from his eyes. This left a purple streak across his brow. At last, he rose and threw down his brush.

"Show us the painting," the judge ordered.

"It's not dry yet," the Painter said.

Ekho bit her lip to keep from smiling. She liked this man, whomever he was, though he had very little sense. He seemed not to know when to be cautious and when to be bold.

"I want to see it!" the king cried.

The Painter shrugged. "Very well," he said. After he lifted the canvas for everyone in the royal box to see, the king, the queen, and the judge gasped. So did the courtiers.

"How dare you?" the king screamed. Flecks of black foam sprayed from the corners of his mouth.

The people craned their necks. Ekho wanted to burst from the crowd to see the painting before the rest of the common folk, but she held herself back. "They might mistake me for one of his apprentices," she thought.

Turning slowly to his left, the Painter showed his final work to the crowd. "Treason!" people shouted. Ekho decided then that he had painted what he had seen, but when she finally saw the painting, she realized that she had guessed wrong. In the middle of the canvas shone a sun. Its left half was purple, its right half yellow. Around it spread the sky, on the left orange, on the right blue. From the bottom of the canvas, a tower stretched toward the sun – a tower that was white on the left and black on the right. She met his eyes and forced herself not to smile. But he did smile, and even as he broke into laughter, she knew that he was doomed.

"If only I could paint," she thought, "I could learn his ways and carry on his work." Then she asked herself, "I? A mere girl?" And then she corrected herself. "My master says I'm a young woman now. Perhaps so, but I'm still powerless. Not like my master and this foolishly brave man."

Facing the royal box once more, the Painter flung his canvas at the judge. Ladies screamed, lords cringed, and archers bent their bows. The painting landed face down in the dust.

"How dare you mock me?" the king snarled.

"You said that I stood between punishment and reward," the Painter replied. "Between death and life. And so I painted with one eye open and one eye shut. Execute half of me, if you can." His laughter rose above the crowd's shrill cries.

With one voice it yelled, "Execute him! Execute him!"

When the king raised a hand, the people fell silent. Archers slackened their bowstrings but kept their arrows notched.

"How well you have them trained," the Painter said. "They might as well be hounds, and you the whipper-in."

The judge rose once more and pulled the white sleeves of his robe back along his forearms. At first, Ekho thought that he was wringing his hands, but then she understood what he was doing: pretending to wash his hands. When he snapped his fingers, a stocky man emerged from the jail. He wore a white hood and trousers but no shirt. Sweat covered his bluish black chest. On his wrists were white leather bands studded with spikes, and he carried a torch. He bowed to the king, turned, and swept the torch in a wide arc so that it knocked the ladder from the scaffold. Dust rose and settled while the crowd held its breath.

At last, the executioner demanded, "Do you have anything to say?"

The Painter asked, "Would you listen if I did?"

"Save your breath, Prisoner," the judge called out. "My Lord Executioner was born deaf."

The Painter sighed. "Of course," he said. "I should have known." He clapped his hands once and let them fall. "It is finished, then."

Ekho nearly cried out, "It can't be!" But, yes, the executioner was jabbing his torch into the wood under the platform. Wisps of smoke began curling out and up. While he circled the scaffold, blue and green flames crackled to life.

The Painter did not flinch. "Is there no one here who sees what I see?" he asked. "Are you all blind?"

Ekho started to weep. "Why are they doing this?" she wondered. "What harm has he done?" She wanted to call out, "I see," but she remained silent. The sky still looked orange to her, the castle tower still white. Tears filled her eyes and the colours ran together. She had to do something – anything – and so she bolted from the crowd.

The Painter turned and smiled at her through waves of heat that rose to surround him. He was shimmering, and though she had never seen what Nevsky called a mirage – an illusion – she knew that this was how it looked. But how could a man be a mirage? Especially this man, who asked her now, "Do you see?"

White smoke mixed with Ekho's tears to sting her eyes. She had to say something – to lie, if need be, but how could she save him with a lie? Shaking her head, she whispered, "No."

The Painter fell to his knees and said, "I've failed, then." He shuddered in the searing flames. He raised clenched fists and shouted, "Oh, God, if I must die for telling the truth, give me the strength to die!"

At last, Ekho remembered that she was not powerless, after all. "Even if I can't save him," she thought, "I can give him the strength he needs." She wiped the tears from her face, took a deep breath, and began to sing.

Everyone fell silent: the whispering courtiers and murmuring crowd. The king turned from the judge, who had been muttering into his ear. Now the only sounds in the courtyard were the crackling of flames and the clear notes of her song. She sang of the courage it took to live for one's beliefs and the strength it took to die; of the happiness when others joined a cause; of the bittersweetness of a martyr's death. She sang pure notes that filled the courtyard and rose, with the smoke, into the sky.

Deaf to the meaning of her words, the people told one another, "She sings alone!"

The executioner approached her, but he was not sure what he should do, and so he looked at the royal box.

"You are forbidden to sing alone!" the king shouted. He clapped his hands over his ears, and his voice rose in pitch. "You may only sing with others! That is my law."

The more he shouted, the stronger Ekho's voice grew, and the more peaceful the Painter looked. The sun began quivering like a purple star, and he reached out for her. When the executioner pinned her arms behind her back, pain wrenched at her shoulders. She thought he might cover her mouth with one of his large hands, but he did not. Despite the pain, she felt as if she could sing forever; as if the whole world could hear her song. But her voice was not rain. When the scaffold collapsed, the Painter vanished in a fountain of blue-green sparks that showered the courtyard.

How the people cheered – until a shriek pierced the air and struck them dumb. Ekho stopped in mid-verse.

Up from the fire rose a hawk. Its beak and talons were a greenish gold and its feathers were blue-green. She had never seen such a bird, so huge that its wings threw sparks the length of the courtyard. Only when the pennons on the castle walls caught fire did she remember why she was here. Home. The princes and the crown. She struggled to break free and the executioner, as terrified now as he was deaf, loosened his grip.

Even as the hawk hovered in front of her and filled the air with its shrieks, it changed colour. Its beak and talons gleamed red-gold. Its feathers flashed an orange-red. And the sparks that flew from its wings onto the people, who screamed while they ran for shelter – these were the colour of sparks in Mir.

Ekho had no time to wonder about this change, for the hawk cried, "Run!"

Colours blurred past her while she fled the castle. No one tried to stop her. They stood, open-mouthed, while the fiery hawk flew overhead and guided her out of the town. Everything else had changed colour, too. Green brick houses were red; grass that had once looked red was green. The lake was blue, as was the sky, and high above the hawk there shone a yellow sun.

When she heard a shout, she glanced back and saw archers in pursuit. They were shooting at the hawk, but their arrows caught fire in its feathers and fell as charred sticks. She ran through the village and up the path next to the falls. They roared, and she shuddered. They looked all the more dangerous now, for they looked real. Mist wet her face while she clambered up the path. "Surely the archers can see me?" she thought. "I'll never make the top." At last, she reached a ledge halfway up the hill and stopped to catch her breath.

"Behind the falls!" the hawk cried. When it plunged through the water, its fire went out with a hiss. But she held back. The water fell so quickly that it might dash her off the ledge and onto the rocks below.

Then the Painter appeared. He stood on the ledge and reached for her with hands that now looked brown. "Come with me," he said. "There's a secret way up the hill."

"Who are you?" she asked, taking an outstretched hand. "Why are you doing this?"

"Later," he said. "Don't look down. And whatever

you do, don't let go."

Despite his warning, she did look down. Far below them, wet rocks waited for her to fall. A whirlpool threatened to suck her broken body out of sight. Hand in hand, she and the Painter moved sideways along the narrow ledge and in behind the falls. How they roared. Icy water fell inches from her eyes and, once, she pulled her hand from the Painter's to wipe her sleeve across her face.

"I told you not to let go," he said, and he once more took her hand.

Halfway along the ledge, he stopped and pointed to an entrance in the cliff. She could see steps hewn into the rock. "Give me your kerchief," he told her. He smiled after she undid the knot under her chin and shook out her chestnut hair. "The kerchief looks red to us," he said, "but the archers will see it as green." Even as he held it in front of him, the falls snatched it from his hand. "They'll find this and think you've drowned. Now, climb!"

"Not until you tell me who you are," she said.

He took her face with both of his hands, and she looked into his eyes. They were no longer colourless. They were dark brown, almost black, with flecks of gold. "Can't you guess?" he asked.

She was about to shake her head. Then her own eyes widened while his craggy, brown face changed shape; while his nose grew even more hooked; while the thumbs that caressed her cheekbones changed back – into feathers.

"Sovah!" she cried.

"Who else?" Drops of water fluttered from his wings onto her face while he hovered. "You're needed at home," he said. He pointed at the steps in the cliff. "Now it's you who must fly!"

CHAPTER 15:
THE MOUNTAINS OF MIR

EVEN AS THE BATTLE BEGAN, NEVSKY SHOUTED, "Stop! In the name of Tsar Leo Dherevo, I order you to stop!"

No one listened to him. Warriors notched arrows while they advanced, and footmen hefted their axes. Boots tramped across the meadow toward the stream. The hearts of men pounded in time with the beat of drums, and this was why he alone heard the laughter rising from the falls.

Dhiavol hovered where the rainbow had once danced. Below him rose a column of steam. His snake's tail – the snake still blind from its battle with Sovah – darted and hissed. Burning saliva dripped down his goat's beard. He landed on the edge of the meadow, and his dragon wings folded behind him. "You've lost, Wise Man," he howled.

"Now, give me the crown."

When the column of steam had appeared, the boyars had stopped to watch it. They could not hear Dhiavol, but they could see the whirling steam. When he yelled, "What are you waiting for?" they heard the roll of drums. When he cried, "Attack!" they heard the blare of horns. They were about to urge their horses onto the frozen stream when Uroth Domah shrieked.

It shrieked with such fury that horses reared. Boyars and warriors fell from their saddles, and their horses trampled both flags – one grey, the other brown. A second shriek sent the royal family scurrying from the mouth of the cave. Even Nevsky shuddered when the cave shrieked for a third time. Then Sovah shot from its mouth. Hooting and screeching, he flapped his wings in the faces of boyars. He pecked at the warriors' breastplates and battered their helmets with his wings. Only after both sides fell back did he attack Dhiavol.

The dragon wings raised Dhiavol into the air. With the ram's horns curving from his head, he tried to butt Sovah aside. Sovah swerved, but the snake tail lashed out to trap him in its coils. Unable to move his wings, he went as limp as a newborn owl. The snake opened its mouth slowly, too slowly, for Sovah struck like lightning. He bit the snake in two.

Dhiavol screamed, and fiery blood gushed from his writhing tail.

Sovah flew out of reach. Not for long, though. He returned to stab with his beak at Dhiavol's haunches.

Nevsky watched this new duel with one eye. With the other, he searched among the women milling in front of the cave. At last, among the princesses in their fur cloaks and red boots – running into sight between Katrina and Elena – Ekho appeared. He called down to her, but she did not look up. She was watching the princes, who still duelled as if nothing had changed; who swung their two-handed swords in long, painful arcs.

"My lords," Nevsky shouted, "stop for a while! Listen to a song while you rest."

The swords, ringing on armour, answered for the princes.

"Attack!" Dhiavol yelled. "Attack, you fools!"

The armies advanced once more. Warriors released their bowstrings, and arrows formed a bristling arch over the princes. Boyars left their horses to leap onto the stream. The ice broke under their weight, yet neither the freezing water nor the slippery stones could stop them.

"Ekho," Nevsky cried, "sing!"

Through the clang of the princes' swords and the

screeching of Sovah and Dhiavol; through the boom of drums, the blare of horns, and the whirr of arrows; through the neighing of horses and the howling of men turned into animals – through all the mad noises of war, Ekho began to sing. No minstrel on Earth could have sung her song. Not even the angels could have strummed chords to accompany her voice. God Himself smiled.

She sang of the birth of children in spring, when leaves bud and flowers bloom; of youths climbing pines in a race to touch the sky; of courtships on warm summer nights and weddings at harvest time, when people give thanks for food and life and love. She sang of long winter nights spent huddled by the fire while winds howl, powerless, outside; of laying the old to rest in beds of frozen earth; of the snow that blankets them; of the sun's triumph over frost; of the promise that comes with spring. She sang of all this, the happy as well as the sad – for without the land, people cannot live, and without its people, the land must weep.

Nevsky also felt happy and sad.

He felt happy when arms grew numb; when warriors no longer bent their bows and footmen no longer raised their axes. The boyars sheathed their swords. Their eyes widened at the sight of two, young men battling for no reason that the boyars could see. The drums and horns had stilled, and so they no longer carried Dhiavol's voice to the ears of men.

He bared his fangs at Ekho, but Sovah blocked his way.

Nevsky felt sad, as well, for she was singing two songs at once. Only he could hear the other song, woven into the first. She sang of sights that no one but he had seen: rivers watering other valleys, mountains sheltering other lands, ships sailing on seas. To the people of Mir, their valley was the world, but she knew now that the world stretched away on all sides. Nevsky thought his heart would burst with joy and grief: joy because her voice made him proud of her; grief because much of what she sang was new to him. "Iron ships," he thought. "How could they not sink? Winged ships? How could they fly?" Not even he, as wise as he was, had seen such wonders in his dreams.

At last, a cheer broke out. He watched boyars, warriors, and footmen leaping the Neva to embrace old friends. They pointed at the duelling princes and laughed with ridicule.

Yet Ikar Napravo and Ivan Levsha fought on. Ekho could banish Dhiavol from the minds of men, but she had no power against his own flesh. The princes swung their dulling swords with tired arms and at last, seeing his army in disarray, Ikar let down his guard.

"Attack!" he shouted at his foremen. "Why do you stand there, rooted like trees?"

Ivan stumbled forward and gashed his brother's side. Even as Ikar cried out, Ivan screamed, for a gash opened in his breastplate. Hot, gritty blood oozed out to stain his brown cloak red. Ivan dropped his sword and clutched at his side. Thinking he could win the duel, Ikar raised his sword and swung it at his brother's neck. But Ivan's head did not fly from his shoulders. Ikar's own head dropped at his feet. Blood bubbled from the severed veins in his neck, and his headless body collapsed.

Ivan picked up his sword. Crazed by the pain in his side and his neck, he hacked at his brother's corpse. "I've won!" he screamed. "I am king!"

Uroth Gorah trembled. Uroth Domah roared like a monster. It shook, and Nevsky lost his footing. Pavel and Preestav helped the women to safety even as boiling water gushed from the cave. It surged like a blue-white tongue to hurtle the princes toward Dhiavol. When the pure water struck him and carried him over the falls, he howled for one last time.

The water rushed into the valley and melted the frozen Reekah. The river boiled through the forest while women and children ran for their homes;

while men ran for the hills. They were seeking protection from their gods, but now the Mountains of Mir began to shake. On the right bank, the statues of Dazhbog and Svarog toppled. The sun god and the god of fiery sky rolled downhill, and when they reached the river, they burst into flames. On the left bank, Velesh the wooden bull and Semur the painted dog rocked from side to side. Velesh's horns cracked and Semur's legs snapped. Rocks tumbled down the mountain to bury Mokosh, the goddess of water. Seeing all this, the men of the countryside fell to their knees to pray to their one true God – He who resembled neither man nor beast. He who had no form.

But even as Mother Reekah ran her furious course, she dried up. Pavel crawled to the edge of the cliff to stare at a muddy road that had once been a river, at piles of rubble that had once been the Mountains of Mir. "The prophecy has come true," he shouted. He rose to say, "The Reekah has dried up and the mountains have fallen down!"

"It can't be," Tserkov said. He hobbled to the top of the falls – to the spot where the falls had been – and his lips moved wordlessly while he gazed at what had once been a valley. The cathedral no longer rose from an island in the middle of a river. There was no river. Women and children staggered across muddy flats and fell on their knees in the shadow of the cross. Men followed without question.

"Oleg," Tserkov cried, "ready my sleigh. Your wife must bake a thousand wafers by sunset, for we celebrate Easter tonight!"

Nevsky clambered down the side of Uroth Domah. "Not yet," he called. "First the people need a ruler." He joined the bishop at the edge of the cliff.

Everyone looked at Tsarevna Katrina. Elena and the six youngest princesses curtsied before readying Katrina for her coronation. With the Neva no longer dividing the meadow, men mingled arm in arm. They stood like this on both sides of a path that had once been a stream, and they grinned at one another. Drums beat a slow march while Katrina followed Oleg, who carried a simple icon of the Virgin and Child. He carried it to the edge of the cliff – the very edge of the only hill that was left in the Kingdom of Mir. Elena and the princesses followed Katrina while Ekho remained near the cave. Only she and Nevsky did not kneel to receive Tserkov's blessing. Still on her knees, Katrina kissed the bishop's hand. Then her people rose as one.

Nevsky planted his staff in the earth. He raised Leo's crown above Katrina, then set it gently on her head. While Tserkov and Ekho exchanged knowing smiles, Sovah read their thoughts: "What an odd

Keeper of the Crown he makes."

Nevsky lifted his arms and announced, "Katrina Lvovna, I charge you in your father's name to rule Mir as wisely as he wanted to himself. May peace prevail until stone floats and straw sinks!" He raised her, kissed her brow, and turned her to face the men of Goroth. "Long live the Queen!" he said.

Pavel shivered with pride. He drew his sword, pointed it at the crown, and called, "Long live the Queen!" So did boyars and warriors and footmen. The wind carried their words across the land and brought back the people's cheers.

"Whoo-ee!" came a cry. "Whoo-ee!" Everyone turned toward Ekho and followed her gaze into the air. Only she and Nevsky understood Sovah, who was crying, "Finished! It is finished, at last." He spun till his brown feathers blurred against the blue sky. Medvyedeetsa and Volcheetsa appeared on the edge of the meadow to watch. When Sovah stopped spinning, he looked like a snow-white dove. He circled once over the meadow, then swooped down the cliff face and along the road to Goroth. When he reached the cathedral, he swooped up past the bell tower, past the copper dome, past the golden cross. Higher and higher he rose. And when a blinding flash lit the afternoon sky, the people of Mir gasped. Sovah had flown into the sun.

No one spoke for a long time.

Ekho blinked back tears.

At last Katrina said, "Master Nevsky, my father named you my foremost boyar. Surely you haven't forgotten? Tell me: what is my first task?"

His thoughts were still on Sovah.

"Master Nevsky," she said.

Recalling his duty to her, he pointed at a spot beyond the cathedral and said, "You must rebuild the palace, Your Majesty. You must build yourself a home."

Katrina gestured for Pavel to come forward. He obeyed her and bowed. "I know that you think I have never marked your loyalty to the crown," she said. "Nor returned your unspoken love. But I have eyes to see, my Lord Virnik. And a heart that feels. You stayed by my side through all the dark days, and not once were you tempted by the spoils that my brothers could have promised. A queen must have a consort to father heirs, for as the Holy Family rules in heaven, so a royal family must rule in Mir."

Happiness lit Pavel's face, and he offered her his arm. "We'll live in my manor till our palace is built," he said. Turning to Tserkov, he asked, "Will you marry us before the sun sets tonight?"

The bishop looked at Nevsky, who nodded.

Then Katrina spoke for all to hear. "Know this,

Master Nevsky: I shall have as the symbol of my rule not my father's two-headed falcon but a snow-white dove in a golden sun, so that our people will always remember Sovah's last flight."

Even as Nevsky bowed, Ekho saw him wipe tears from his eyes. Everyone left him then, and for a time he stood alone. After she joined him, he placed an arm about her shoulder and leaned on his staff. Neither of them spoke. They watched what had once been two armies mingle to file downhill, to descend on either side of what had once been falls. Falls in whose spray a rainbow had danced.

At the foot of the hill, Katrina mounted her horse. She led her court and the once blind men of Goroth – all of them – back to their homes. The snow melted under her horse's hooves, and this became her promise to the people of Mir: that however harsh the winter, it would always be followed by spring. Bear cubs and wolf cubs tumbled from dens and lairs; buds appeared on trees; crocuses bloomed in her wake. And just as sadness must follow joy and joy must follow sadness, the sun triumphed once again in its never-ending battle with frost.

TO END:

THE LEGEND OF BYELLEEYE FALLS

FOR THE THIRD AND FINAL TIME, EVEN AS THE minstrel strummed a flourish on his harp, we pounded on tables with our cups. The hounds woke to bark and bay. We filled the hall with so much noise that the banners rippled until the embroidered eagles fluttered their wings. He waved off our applause, but while he placed his harp at his feet, a smile of self-congratulation – no, of gratitude – curved his lips. Only our queen remained silent, apparently unmoved on her gossamer-curtained throne.

The steward, a man who would not stoop to pet a hound – he was that grudging with both wine and affection – gathered the coins we tossed for the minstrel. Silver and gold clinked and rolled and came to rest on the flagstones. When a foreign merchant insisted that he had no purse — that he had yet to receive a warrant from me to ply his wares — his fellows shamed him into tugging a ring off one of his meaty fingers. He added the ring to the coins the steward was gathering. Then, standing in front of the minstrel, the steward held his hands high above the blind man's head and let the treasure cascade into his lap.

Sunlight glinted off the coins. The tale had lasted all night and yet I wanted to hear more, because the hissing of the coins reminded me of Byelleeye Falls. "A fine tale," I said, speaking for the entire court. Feeling the need to say more, I concluded with, "A simple tale, and simply told."

Certain courtiers, chief among them my betrothed, frowned in disagreement with my conclusion. How sure I was of all that I said in that long-ago time. How sure I sounded, at least.

Much later, I saw that the simplicity of the minstrel's tale and of its telling were of little consequence. He had done what we had hoped. He had transported us out of our everyday lives with a living, breathing tale and brought us back to lives that would never be the same. Not that he had promised any of this, but while I sat there exchanging conciliatory glances with my beloved, how could I have known that our lives would, indeed, be forever changed? Or how soon. And this by a man with a harp, a staff, a sack, and a single story to his name.

At last he said, "My thanks, Lady Chancellor. From you, that is no doubt high praise."

"You are most welcome," I said coldly. Then, to mollify him, "But what of the Legend of Byelleeye Falls? 'If two lovers pass hand in hand –'" I stopped to recall the rest of the legend and he quickly asked, "Are you sure you want to know?"

At this everyone – especially the keeper, who had regaled us with his own, fanciful epilogue – looked surprised.

"Why would we not?" I said. "Tell us! How many sons were born to Ekho and her wise man?"

The minstrel started as if I had pierced him with words that could draw blood. As if my tongue were a swiftly uncurling blade.

"Yes, tell us!" lords and ladies cried. So did other courtiers, the merchants, and the servants, as well – though they risked the steward's wrath over such presumption. Many of our number yawned or stretched, yet no one made for bed.

The old man took up his harp with some effort, balanced it on his left knee, and once again faced the throne. "Very well," he said. "Only remember – I tried to spare you an unhappy ending."

"Unhappy, how?" I wondered. The kingdom had

been saved. Katrina had inherited the crown. True, Sovah had left, but Ekho and Nevsky could marry at last. She would remove his boots not as a daughter but as a bride.

The minstrel strummed a chord more suited to a lament than a hymn of praise. Of exultation for the triumph of sun over frost. Still, that falling chord transported us, for one last time, to the Kingdom of Mir.

NEVSKY STOOD with his arm about Ekho's shoulder for some time. He had missed her during her time in that other world, and he wanted to hold her forever. Silently, they watched the celebrations in the forest below. Fires roared near village wells, and the sounds of music and dancing filled the warming air. For the first time since Leo's death, the people had a reason to be merry, but when Nevsky turned to look at Uroth Domah, he felt sad.

The cave no longer grinned. The boiling water had smashed its fangs, had carried away the table and chairs, the cupboards and benches, the beds, and the bearskin rug. The clay stove lay in a heap, and torn curtains hung in the cave's mouth. He and Ekho followed the muddy path that had once been a stream back to what had once been a home. When she began searching for dishes, candles, and their few books, he said, "Don't worry. I'll build a sturdy pine cabin in the forest. Or ask Katrina for a favour. Yes, for your sake, I'll ask for a manor in the countryside and a house in Goroth." He laughed. "What was I thinking of? The queen's foremost boyar and his lady can't live in the forest!"

When he touched Ekho's shoulder to bid her to rise, she did so without looking at him. "If it's only for my sake," she said, "don't ask any favours. I can't marry you now."

He stared at her. "What?" he asked.

"I said –"

"I heard what you said. But we're betrothed!"

She still refused to look at him. "And you said we would marry when bridges once more spanned the Reekah. There is no river, so what need is there for bridges?"

He tugged at his beard in astonishment; at the way she was flinging his words back at him. "But we must marry," he said. "Have you forgotten the legend? If two lovers pass hand in hand behind Byelleeye Falls, they will live in peace and enter heaven together."

She faced him at last. "No, Master," she said. "It

is you who has forgotten. If two lovers pass hand in hand behind the falls without once losing sight of the rainbow, they will live in peace and enter heaven together. I walked in that backward world with the Painter, with Sovah, not with you. And I saw no rainbow. Also, once, when I grew frightened, I released his hand."

"But Sovah was part of me," Nevsky said. "He was the bird that flew while the man could only walk. My spirit went with you beyond the door."

"Then your spirit must marry mine."

At this, he slapped his brow. "Where is the girl I raised?" he asked, as if the forest could answer. "Not only has she grown up overnight, but she also claims that she doesn't need me now!" He told her, "If I hadn't given you the key, Mir would have gone to hell in flames, but Uroth Domah would have remained untouched." He looked at the muddy ground and said, "We could have lived happily then."

Ekho sat on a rock near the cave's mouth and clasped her hands in her lap. "I know you too well," she said. "You despised people like the butcher and the milkmaid for their superstitions and men like Starik for clinging to the past, but in your heart you cared for them. If you really had turned your back on Mir, you could never have forgiven yourself. Why, you nearly went mad searching for the key that would lighten their dark days. Can't you find happiness in knowing that you did your duty?" With her head bent, with her hands covering her face, she began to weep. Through her tears, she said, "Let's not part so sadly."

He looked up from the mud at his feet. "What now?" he asked. "Why should we part?"

"Because I've finished my work here. The world outside needs me more than our people do. You will advise Katrina, marry one of her sisters, and –"

He threw down his staff and paced in front of the cave. "You sang of life and land and love," he reminded her. Then he raised his arms, threw back his head, and shouted at the sky, "This is not what should have come to pass!"

"Perhaps not, Master," she said, "and yet it has. I sang so the people would open their eyes, though you and I both know truths that few people want to hear. The land is cruel as well as kind. The happiest life is too short, and the saddest life too long. It's our duty as those who see, as masters of whatever is this art that we practise, to live apart from others so that we never lose sight of such truths. And the hardest truth of all –" Here her voice dropped. " – is that we don't need each other. Not any more."

"I'm no longer your master," he said angrily. "You

stopped learning from me when you walked through that door." He laughed and pounded a clenched fist into his palm. "With the key I gave you, fool that I was!" He mused on this for a while. Then, one last time, he tried to keep her for himself. Even as he did this, he knew that he was no longer acting like a wise man, but after all that they had shared, how could he not try? "Let's get ready," he said. "We'll both leave Mir."

"No!" she cried. Wiping the tears from her face, she rose. "Why do you make me hurt you like this? How could I help other people if we were happy together? It's our lot to grieve while helping others find –"

"Aha!" he exclaimed. Even as he rubbed his palms, he ignored a sudden puckering on the backs of his hands. He also ignored a twitch that pulled at his left eye while the skin tightened across his cheek. He was changing into a man who had survived a childhood fire, but there was much that he no longer saw and even more that he no longer understood. "You're wrong for once," he said. "You're twisting words the way I used to twist them against Starik and Ikar and Ivan. Words that sound very fine but are worse than empty. Words that are false."

"It's our lot to grieve," she repeated, "and when at last we find joy, we'll relish it all the more. Let me go,

Sasha! Too much has changed. Let me choose my own path, just as you let Sovah choose his."

This was the final blow: not her mentioning Sovah, but her speaking a name she should not have known. "Sasha?" he asked. How strange it sounded after all these years, and how strange his face and hands felt. He asked the forest, "Am I no longer Nevsky? Am I not the wise man who lived at the source of a stream called the Neva? Am I not even Dhurak, the holy fool?" He tried to harden his heart against the girl he had raised – against the wise young woman she had become – but how could he, when he loved her more than life itself?

He looked at the cave, hollowed out now, and the drying mud of the stream. "She's right," he said. "Too much has changed. Worst of all, I'm not as wise as I once was. I've lost all my powers. To her." He looked at the sun and shook his head. "No, that's not true. Sovah was the one with the power. If only he would come back." A yellow spot blazed in Nevsky's eyes. He thought that by staring at the sun, he could bring back not only Sovah but also the happy times they had shared. Then he sighed, and his chin dropped till his beard scratched at his throat, but no matter where he looked or how often he blinked, he could not escape the glare of a sun that looked purple to him now, not yellow. A purple that was fading to black.

He stumbled into the cave and cried, "Ekho?" No one answered him. He fell against a wall of stones and found the passage blocked. Steadying himself and turning, he pressed his fingertips against his eyelids, then opened his eyes. Even as he groped his way out of the cave and found his staff by feel — even as he crossed a meadow that stretched to the ends of the earth — he saw that he had lost more than magical powers and wisdom, more than Sovah and Ekho. He had lost his sight, as well.

"YOU!" That single word, shouted in the hall, hung over the minstrel like a sentence. Only when he shook his head sadly did I realize that the word had burst from my own mouth. And that I stood pointing at him as if I were a judge and he the accused.

"No, Lady Chancellor," he said. "My pardons if I misled you." He placed his harp on the floor and groped for the sack. After he straightened, he fumbled with the drawstring.

My arm fell as heavily to my side as I did into my chair. Slouched in confusion, I watched him fill the sack with coins, a few at a time, and with all eyes but his upon me, I felt like a fool. I would have believed anything just then, so I heard what he wanted me to hear when he paused to say, "I am not Nevsky."

Then he finished filling the sack with coins and that one merchant's ring. No one moved or made a sound until he pulled the drawstring taut. At last he declared, "I am plain old Sasha, who does not even bear his father's name – no Mikhailovich, no Ivanovich – because, even as the villagers of Dherevnia forgot the orphan they had once housed and fed, so he forgot the parents he surely must have loved."

I expected exclamations of pity, but still no one spoke – neither courtier nor merchant nor servant – because the minstrel was weaving a different spell than the one he had woven with his tale. He addressed not the old queen, as he had for much of the night. He addressed me alone. And though I relished being the centre of attention when I spoke for her, I wished that he would address some other personage in that hall. Unsure of what emotions to betray, I composed my face so that I appeared unmoved by what I now heard. As if my heart were a stone.

"Plain old Sasha," he repeated. "I was Nevsky, yes, though I can't prove it, and what need is there for proof? I was once-upon-a-wise-man in a once-upon-a-land. But I no longer have magical powers. Nor do I miss them, though I do miss the use of my eyes. As all of you can see, I carry a pouch that once held a crown. I bear my harp like a cross. I walk with the aid of a staff. When the air grows damp, my scarred hands ache, and my face throbs like a drum. How can such a man call himself Nevsky? Or even the holy fool, Dhurak?"

He tucked the knot of the drawstring into his belt. He picked up the harp and cradled it in the crook of his left arm. He planted the end of the staff on a flagstone, then struggled to his feet. He was halfway to the door when the lady-in-waiting, no doubt sent by the queen, approached him. They stopped to exchange a few low words. He nodded gratefully toward what he thought was the throne, but he was facing me.

"For seven times seven years," he said, "I have wandered from east to west while making my way from north to south. I have come at last to the Middle Earth Sea, which lies closer to the sun than the Reekah and the Neva once flowed. Finally, I have reached a temperate land, where the sun has no need to battle frost. Everywhere I have stopped, I have told this tale." Brightening suddenly, he declared, "As I've said, it's the only tale I know, so you see why I keep moving on!" He smiled, but no one smiled with him, and he could not have seen them if they had.

"On every road I've travelled," he said, "I have asked about Ekho. Sometimes I heard how she helped kingdoms find their peace. Sometimes I lost her trail for year upon year. And so I now ask you what I have asked so many times in so many places and on so many mornings like this. Have any of you seen her? Have you perhaps at least heard of her during your own travels?"

The foreign merchants shrugged.

The rest of us looked toward the old queen, who sat behind her gossamer curtain. Who, as she had throughout the night, hung on his every word. She was no longer toying with the ring on her right hand. That precious ring with its symbol of her reign. Not a blue-green eagle, after all – nor even a hawk – but a blue-green bird that had risen from flames into an orange sky. A firebird. She toyed not with this ring but with a strand of hair as silver as the moon. Hair that had once been the colour of chestnut. With her hazel eyes, she looked at me now, as did the keeper, the steward, and my betrothed with their own worried eyes. As did every courtier and servant and even, I fancied, the hounds. Yes, even they knew the answer to the minstrel's question, but it was left for me to speak – not only for our queen but also for our people, to whom she truly was the sun with its life-giving rays.

And so I rose once more and stiffened my back. When I silenced my clinking chain of office by pressing my palm against my breast, I no doubt looked as if I were swearing an oath. "We have never seen her," I declared. Compelled to say more, as always, I added, "Nor had we ever heard her name until we heard your tale." This much, at least, was true.

He nodded while I spoke, though whether he knew that I was lying – and that this alone saddened him – I cannot say. But he realized that he had been facing the head table and not the throne. He turned to his right. "And you, O Phantom Queen?" he asked. "You, who ride veiled through your land, and whose voice is heard only by those who serve at court, have you seen my Ekho? Or heard of her?"

How long I held my breath, I do not know. I only know that I watched her toying with that strand of hair – watched the symbol of her reign glint in the early morning light that pierced the gossamer curtain – and I prayed that she would not speak.

She did not, and even now I cannot decide whether I felt gladness or dismay. I often wonder what might have occurred had she risen from her throne; had she reached toward him while singing of life and land and love; had she effected a reunion that would have moved us to tears. But this was not the ending that had been ordained for their story. She clasped her hands in her lap and sat motionless. She waited to see what he might do next. To hear what else he might say.

He sighed, though again, whether he knew that she was hiding something – hiding the truth, hiding herself – I cannot say. His chin dropped so that had he not been blind, he could have seen the dust of our winding southern roads on his colourless shoes. He turned slowly so that he faced me once more. So that he was again two men – on the right, aged yet whole; on the left, painfully scarred. "My search is finished," he said. "For now. Yours is the last of the hundred kingdoms between the dancing green northern lights and the Middle Earth Sea. Today I shall sail to its southern shore. I have heard that another hundred kingdoms lie there. And beyond. I doubt that I shall live long enough to visit them all, but your generosity will pay for my crossing. And more. I thank you for this. Your Majesty," he declared. "Lady Chancellor, my lords, ladies, and merchants and all of you courtly servants, I bid you farewell."

So saying, he pounded his staff on the floor. Not three times, as he had in order to break loose the southern tip of Goroth. Only once. Yet this was enough to jar the dirt of the road from his staff. We saw that its surface was not smooth, after all. Even as a circle of dusty flakes formed at the foot of the staff, symbols appeared in the ashwood, just as images had appeared on the sound box of his harp. But I was not imagining what now emerged – deeply etched symbols that we could see but that he could only feel. There were common ones like stars and moons, lightning bolts and snakes. There were also scorpions, which could not have thrived in his cold northern land.

Then, oblivious of how much he had revealed, he left us.

How weary I felt, as if I had spent the entire night battling demons in some distant land and now could have slept for days. The rest of the court must have felt as I did. Lords and ladies went to their beds. Even the keeper was too sleepy – no, too affected by emotion – to compose some witty commentary. My betrothed bowed when I glanced in his direction, but I did not bid him good night. Or good morning. Only the foreign merchants, who speculated on where the minstrel might find the love he had lost – only they chattered. They asked me to convey their thanks to our queen for her hospitality, and I muttered, "Yes, yes," while I watched her every move.

In those days, the wall behind the throne was a frescoed mural that is now covered with muslin over silk. I ordered this done because the mural had been retouched so often during the first year of my reign that the resulting patchwork displeased me. Yet in the old queen's day, that mural glowed in blues and greens and golds. It was a panorama of our capital city as seen from the southern approach. On the left, to the west, was the port, harbouring vessels that have anchored here over the centuries – triremes and other galleys with banks of bristling oars; long ships with square sails, graceful hulls, and dragon's head prows; and merchant vessels with triangular, lanteen sails. What histories this port could relate if riggings were harps and oars were tongues.

On the right, to the east, rose our palace on a cliff from which a fortress once commanded the approach. Set into the painted cliff, directly behind the throne, was a door whose seams were almost invisible. This door allowed our queen to climb a staircase that led – and still does lead – to the palatial apartments on the floor above the hall. It was through this door that she now vanished, but first she cast me a look that told me where she was bound. Not to her own chambers but to mine.

"Counsel, now?" I wondered.

After the merchants left, I slipped behind the curtain, skirted the throne, let myself in by the painted door, and climbed a winding staircase. This led me to a hallway along whose length other doors opened into a series of apartments. These doors still open into apartments – my own, my husband's, my daughter's, and her husband's – but the hallway is no longer a secret. Nor is it as dark as it once was, for I have ordered it widened so that it does not feel like the passageway of olden times. Like a passage that joined two caves. I entered my chambers, from which windows and a balcony afforded views of the sea. Here I found our queen awaiting me in my reading room.

The queen, Her Majesty – Ekho did not speak.

Watching her wander about the room, watching her admire the handful of books I then owned and the flowers on a windowsill, I easily saw her as she must have looked fifty years before, in a linen gown and apron, with her hair gathered by a silver comb – while she stood at the top of a waterfall and looked out over a troubled land. Or did I merely see a portrait that the minstrel, that Nevsky-Dhurak – that Sasha had painted with his words?

At last she asked me, "Why did you lie?"

"I had no choice," I said. "I was afraid that he would take you from us."

Facing the window, she reached for a parched rose that drooped among wildflowers wilting in an earthenware vase. She held the rose to the light and began to hum. I watched, entranced, while the rose bloomed. While she gave it new life just as she gave every good and living thing that heard her songs new life. The wildflowers bloomed, as well. Holding the rose, which was dewy now, she turned from the window and said, "Nevsky tried to keep me for himself."

"Ekho —" I began. Then I remembered my place. "Your Majesty," I said, "when you arrived in our land, we aristocrats were like the boyars of Mir. We quarrelled among ourselves, so blinded that we couldn't see the beauty of our land or of the sea. We were no better than animals. Worse, my father said. Animals give back to the land while too many men only take. You taught us to preserve what we had instead of destroying it. You commanded the transformation of a fortress into a palace. You —"

"Words," she said. She placed the rose on my reading stand. "Only words. We both know that I can't live forever. Before long, our people will crown a new ruler, and everyone hopes that she will be a thoughtful woman who was once a less-than-thoughtful chancellor." Ekho laced her fingers and turned her back on me. Then she said, "How quaint," and laughed softly. "A virgin queen. Are there many others, do you think?" She peered out a window — not west toward the port but straight ahead toward a distant, invisible shore. "I must also sail south."

"Wait for the sea to calm," I cautioned her. "It's the season of storms." But she did not want to hear such things. She was hearing a voice more compelling than my own.

"He will have reached our ship by now," she declared, "though he no doubt thinks it awaits the tide." She faced me once more and said, "I never should have left him. For a few years, perhaps, so that I could become sufficient unto myself, but forever? I was wrong when I said that it's our lot to grieve while making others happy. Was I trying to be wise or hoping to become a saint? And to think that, for some time, I hoped I had taught him a lesson – by spurning him the way he had spurned the villagers who had once looked after him. But he was far kinder to me than they had ever been to him. Oh, how much I learned beyond the door that night. And how little I knew."

She looked at the book that lay open on my reading stand. It was one whose copying, illumination, and binding I had commissioned to mark my appointment as chancellor – *The Virgin Mary's Journey Through the Inferno.*

"Beware the power of words," Ekho said. "I wonder whether Katrina, the Queen of Mir, learned to beware them, as well. Or how soon her descendants will feel their double edge."

"Why should they?" I asked. "Peace came at last to Mir."

"For a while, perhaps," Ekho said. "Only a while, for my master unwittingly cursed its people even as he blessed them." She sighed – not with impatience over my slowness to grasp her meaning but with sorrow for the land she had once saved. "'Before any woman can wear our tsar's crown,'" she prompted.

"'The Reekah must dry up and the mountains fall down,'" I finished for her. "Everyone thought it was impossible, but it happened, and a woman did become tsaritsa. Did become queen."

Ekho nodded. "And when my master crowned Katrina, he said, 'May peace prevail until stone floats and straw sinks.' How grand it sounded then, but if the very Mountains of Mir could fall –"

"– then one day," I said, feeling a shiver in my heart, "stone will float and straw will sink." It was a shiver of pride that I had learned yet another lesson. And of dread for the people of Mir.

She nodded again – not with sadness, but over the need for sadness to follow joy. And if sadness must follow joy, and if a magical kingdom like Mir should once again lose sight of peace, are any of our lands truly safe from descending into madness? However civilized – no, however civil – we act.

Forgive me, I digress. But I know something now. While it may indeed be old age that causes me to overlook certain things – such as your own desire for my tale to end – it is not old age that causes me to digress. It is fear. I am afraid that if my own tale should draw to a close, my reign must also end, and Death himself will come for me one of these nights. What cowards we mortals are, at times. True, I approached my throne with shaky steps, but I have sat on it for so long – though without Ekho's unstudied grace or her magical power – that I cannot imagine anyone else on this same throne. Not even my beloved daughter.

Ekho looked again at the sea, and I reached for the rose. A thorn pricked my finger at once – the fourth finger of my right hand. I sucked on my wound while watching her remove the two royal rings. How often I had imagined wearing them. And before I could protest – before I could claim that I was not ready to bear such precious burdens – the ring from her left hand graced my own left hand. This was the tarnished ring my father had given her after he had crowned her queen. The ring that bore the symbol of our dead king – two swords crossed on a field the colour of our forefathers' blood. The ring that, later, I could not remove too soon. And before I could draw away, the ring from her right hand graced my own right hand. This was the jewelled ring that bore the firebird – the symbol of her reign and, from that moment on, the symbol of my own.

At last, I did protest, "I'm not ready!"

She touched my face as if she were comforting a child. "You will never be ready," she said. "And not only because you have lived in my shadow for so long. But how can you deny yourself your destiny? The crown is yours, at last. This is what you have wanted for years, and you must make of it what you will. Rule well, Lady Chancellor. Rule well, my queen."

Then she was gone, through the door that led to the once secret hallway, into her chambers, and out again. Few people saw her leave. The coachman who drove her to the port did tell us one thing that struck him as odd. She wore a necklace of bear's teeth from which dangled an iron key. I cannot guess where she had kept it hidden during all her years on the throne, but I do wonder how often she tied on that necklace and looked in a mirror at her younger self. How often she pondered what little she had brought with her from Uroth Gorah. And all that she had left.

WHAT I HAVE TOLD YOU THUS FAR took place long ago, before I married, before I bore a princess, and before I found a certain amount of wisdom in the middle years of my life. I have ruled as wisely as I could. There may have been better rulers on Earth, but I suspect that none have been more thoughtful than I. As for my husband, there are times I have wished he had the strength of a prince without the weakness of a man. Perhaps I have expected too much. Perhaps I have asked questions when I should have decided, or changed my mind when I should have stayed the course. Or perhaps I simply let the heart of a woman rule the mind of a queen. One thing I do know is that whenever I weary of the crown I bear, the firebird on my ring reminds me of Nevsky's tale and of the lessons I learned from Ekho without once learning why we, of all peoples, should have been so blessed. How quickly that fateful night passed – far more quickly than this long night. Than most of my nights now, while I roam hallways and halls. While I stand on my balcony and wish that the stars could sing me to sleep with the music of the spheres.

No one knows what happened to Ekho and

Nevsky. Some claim that their ship sank in a storm. Others claim that they live in a southern land whose people are as dark as the shadows they cast. Yet, whatever people say, they agree on this much. There was never such a time in this land as when the old queen ruled – that once and perfect queen – and though the present queen seems kind enough in her dotty old age, surely the time has come for her to relinquish the crown? Yes, the time has come. Later this morning, I shall make one last proclamation. My daughter will be pleased. Perhaps, though, when I pass to her this ring with its jewelled firebird, she too will protest, "I'm not ready," and I will touch her face.

Now, at last, to end.

Here I stand on my balcony as I do each morning before I descend to hold court. And each morning, I hear laughter on the shore below the cliff. Three figures emerge from a mist where there should be no mist. One I know to be Nevsky. Not the blind old minstrel I met but a bearded young man. Another I know to be Ekho. Not the silver-haired queen whose voice enchanted us, but a maiden who skips beside him. Nevsky calls to creatures I cannot see – a bear and a wolf, perhaps – and Ekho hums a tune I cannot hear. Above them, an owl named Sovah sets the seabirds to laughing with his *Whoo*s. Then the sun rises over this mediterranean sea, and all three figures vanish with the mist.

To tell the truth, I have never seen this, not once, but it is an old woman's privilege to dream such dreams. To mould the truth into what she would like it to be. This much I know. God in His mercy reunited Ekho and her wise man. They did pass behind the falls, if only in spirit, and even if they did lose sight of the rainbow from their own, magical world, that rainbow danced in their mind's eye. They may not have lived in peace for long, but they entered heaven together. I am sure of it. And this, too, I know. Nevsky is wise once more, as wise as the Ekho who ruled here as the Phantom Queen, and by leaving us for him, she rekindled their love. This above all, my friends. This, above all. For as Nevsky discovered by teaching her what little he knew, and as Ekho often asked me – while she must have dreamt of halcyon days in their once-upon-a-land –

Of what use is wisdom without love?

ACKNOWLEDGEMENTS

AT LEAST FOUR PEOPLE HELPED ME WRITE THIS BOOK. Geoffrey Ursell urged me to transform a story into a novel and, much later, edited the novel for publication. Jack Hodgins took me on as an apprentice long before I was ready to learn from a master. Pat Krause commented on early revisions to the manuscript. And my wife, Shelley Sopher, commented on the next to last draft. All this took some twenty-four years, more off than on, from 1978 until 2002. What can I say except that I can be slow? Mind you, someone once asked a famous writer how long it takes to write a good book and he said something like, "Just as long as it takes to write a bad book."

Over the years, I also received financial support that helped this project along: a creative grant from the Saskatchewan Arts Board; three appointments as a writer-in-residence – in The University of Calgary's Markin-Flanagan Distinguished Writers Programme and, with support from The Canada Council for the Arts, at Regina Public Library and at McMaster University's Department of English; and, at different times, two subsidies from The Banff Centre for the Arts to work in its Leighton Studios – where I retreat from the world so that I can recreate the world.

ABOUT THE AUTHOR

VEN BEGAMUDRÉ has published *Isaac Brock: Larger than Life*, a biography for young adults and adults; a novel, *Van de Graaff Days;* two short story collections, *Laterna Magika* and *A Planet of Eccentrics;* and a novella, *Sacrifices.* He also has numerous short stories, essays, poems, and public readings to his credit. A number of his books, short fiction and non-fiction pieces have won national awards.

Born in Bangalore, in southern India, Ven Begamudré has lived in Canada since he was six. He has a public administration degree from Carleton University, and an MFA in Creative Writing from Warren Wilson College in North Carolina. He makes his home in Regina.